"You won't be going anywhere by yourself,"

Tony told Faith. "At least, not yet."

"I gave you all the information I could," she protested. "And I won't tell the police what you're up to."

"Yeah, right. Lying to the authorities. I can see it now. You'd better stick close to me," he added. "You never know what you might run into trying to hitch a ride home."

"That's ridiculous." Not to mention incredibly high-handed of him! Still, warmth spiraled through her.

Faith glanced away from Tony's intriguing profile and tried to concentrate on the outrageousness of his actions.

How dare he taunt her—not to mention keep her hostage!

Dear Reader,

This month, Silhouette Romance brings you six wonderful new love stories—guaranteed to keep your summer sizzling! Starting with a terrific FABULOUS FATHER by Arlene James. A *Mail-order Brood* was not what Leon Paradise was expecting when he asked Cassie Esterbridge to be his wife. So naturally the handsome rancher was shocked when he discovered that his mail-order bride came with a ready-made family!

Favorite author Suzanne Carey knows the kinds of stories Romance readers love. And this month, Ms. Carey doesn't disappoint. *The Male Animal* is a humorous tale of a couple who discover love—in the midst of their divorce.

The fun continues as Marie Ferrarella brings us another delightful tale from her Baby's Choice series—where matchmaking babies bring together their unsuspecting parents.

In an exciting new trilogy from Sandra Steffen, the Harris brothers vow that no woman will ever tie them down. But their WEDDING WAGER doesn't stand a chance against love. This month, a confirmed bachelor suddenly becomes a single father—and a more-than-willing groom—in *Bachelor Daddy*.

Rounding out the month, Jeanne Rose combines the thrill of the chase with the excitement of romance in *Love on the Run*. And *The Bridal Path* is filled with secrets—and passion—as Alaina Hawthorne spins a tale of love under false pretenses.

I hope you'll join us in the coming months for more great books from Elizabeth August, Kasey Michaels and Helen Myers.

Until then—

Happy Reading!

Anne Canadeo
Senior Editor

Please address questions and book requests to:
Silhouette Reader Service
U.S.: 3010 Walden Ave., P.O. Box 1325, Buffalo, NY 14269
Canadian: P.O. Box 609, Fort Erie, Ont. L2A 5X3

LOVE ON THE RUN

Jeanne Rose

ROMANCE™

Published by Silhouette Books

America's Publisher of Contemporary Romance

Dedicated to Strike the Gold, 1991 Kentucky Derby winner,
and to all Thoroughbreds, athletes of beauty and grace
who race their hearts out for our pleasure.

With special thanks to:

Teri Holopoff & Terry's Red Colors,
Charlie Livesay & The Flying I Stables,
Arlington International Racecourse
The Kentucky Derby Museum
Nicholas P. Zito Racing Stable

 SILHOUETTE BOOKS

ISBN 0-373-19027-1

LOVE ON THE RUN

Books by Jeanne Rose

Silhouette Romance

Believing in Angels #913
Love on the Run #1027

Silhouette Shadows

The Prince of Air and Darkness #26

JEANNE ROSE

is the newest pseudonym of Patricia Pinianski and Linda Sweeney. The Chicagoans have been a team since 1982, when they met in a writing class. Now Linda teaches writing at two suburban community colleges and works for *Writer's Digest,* while Patricia makes writing her full-time focus. Patricia and Linda are happy they can combine their fascination with the mysterious and magical with their belief in the triumph of love. Patricia and Linda are also known as Lynn Patrick, and Patricia writes as Patricia Rosemoor.

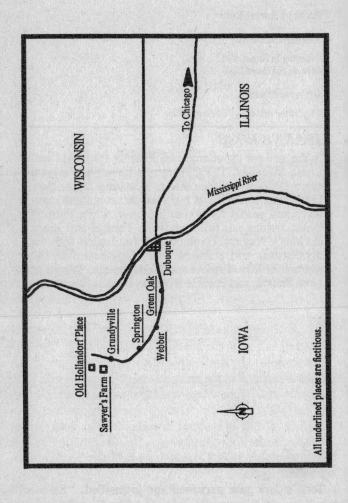

WISCONSIN

ILLINOIS

IOWA

To Chicago

Mississippi River

Dubuque

Green Oak

Webber

Springton

Grundyville

Old Hollandorf Place

Sawyer's Farm

All underlined places are fictitious.

Chapter One

Faith Murray switched on the television news and headed back into her closet-sized kitchen. After a Saturday afternoon of overtime at the Chicago insurance company where she worked, she was now focused on dinner. She listened to the day's events with half an ear until the sports announcer caught her interest.

"True Heart, winner of this year's Kentucky Derby, is stabled right here in the northwest suburbs...."

Removing a chicken potpie from the microwave, Faith paused and stared at the screen. Behind the announcer were the barns of Rolling Meadows Racecourse and beside him was Tony D'Angelo, True Heart's charismatic trainer.

"Some people have been disappointed in your horse, Tony," said the sports announcer. "He's zero for five and hasn't won since May. Do you think he'll ever find the winner's circle again?"

Tony's dark gaze narrowed and intensified. "Sure he'll win," he said, his gravelly voice tinged by East Coast braggadocio. "T.H. is a great horse, full of heart. We've just had some bad luck, poor post positions. But he'll come through again. You can count on it."

"Well, you've heard it here...almost from the horse's mouth," joked the announcer as the coverage switched to baseball.

Concerned for True Heart's losing streak, Faith frowned and turned the volume down. Then she felt silly. The horse would be fine whether he won another race or not. She wasn't even sure why she felt so connected to the gritty chestnut who'd made a charge from dead last to circle the field and come flying across the finish line first in the country's premier Thoroughbred race.

Not that she'd seen the Kentucky Derby in person. Her seat had been the sleeper couch in front of the television. The colt's victory had come as a surprise to the commentators; True Heart had certainly not been the favorite.

Faith knew how it felt to be a long shot, to have the odds stacked against her. But she was determined that her own courage and heart would help her win big someday.

Thinking about her goals—the business degree for which she'd been going to school part-time for eight years, a better job than her insurance adjuster position, a larger apartment with a view, vacations to beautiful spots where she could enjoy nature—Faith dumped the potpie on a plate and returned to the couch. The table was too loaded with schoolbooks to allow space for meals. From beneath it, her calico cat peeked out, then came running to brush against her legs.

"Lucy, you already had your supper." Though from the cat's pitiful meowing, one wouldn't think so. "Let me eat in peace."

But as Lucy rose on the tippy-tips of her pretty white paws and assumed her best woebegone expression, Faith caved in and gave the cat a chunk of chicken.

Meanwhile, still thinking about True Heart, Faith slid a videotaped replay of the derby into her VCR so she could watch as she ate. She'd watched up to the part where the horse's owners and Tony D'Angelo were screaming themselves hoarse with the joy of victory when a loud knock came at the door.

"Open up, it's Audra!"

Faith paused the tape to let in her next-door neighbor. Trailing a purple gauzy scarf that drooped lower than the hem of her black spandex miniskirt, Audra sailed into the apartment and raised her eyebrows at the television screen.

"Wow, some hunk!"

Faith glanced at the close-up of Tony D'Angelo. Probably thirty-five or so, he was intriguingly tough-looking, with a scarred eyebrow and slightly crooked nose. "He's not bad," she hedged, not wanting Audra to think she worshiped celebrities.

"Who is he, anyway?"

"Oh...uh, a horse trainer."

"You're watching that silly horse race again?"

"I enjoy watching Thoroughbreds run," said Faith a bit defensively. "The horses always look so free."

Audra snorted, and the many earrings piercing her ears danced up and down. "Racehorses don't have any freedom. They spend most of their time locked up in a stall. I thought you and I agreed on animal rights."

"I *do* agree with most of your ideas. But I don't think anybody would mistreat a horse who's worth so much money." Especially not Tony, Faith told herself, certain from the interviews she'd seen and read that he had integrity. She pointed out, "I was the first one to sign your petition."

A vociferous spokeswoman for Animals Were Here Before Us, Audra had drafted a bill of rights urging everyone who worked with animals to treat them with respect.

"True. I sent copies to all the local racetracks and their personnel."

"Did you see the way he ran the rest of them down?" came Tony D'Angelo's voice from the television set as the video recorder shifted back into play. In the background, True Heart—known to fans as T.H.—nipped at one of his owners playfully, causing the man to pull away. Tony D'Angelo enthused, "I've got the greatest horse in the world!"

Audra widened her eyes in appreciation. "Hey, sexy voice."

While Faith agreed, she didn't say so. Instead, she turned off the recorder and television. "So, what's up?"

"You know we're going to Nefertiti's tonight," Audra said, referring to a local dance club. She frowned at Faith's white blouse and plain gray pants. "You're not wearing that, are you?"

"To be truthful, I forgot."

Although both women were twenty-eight, Faith didn't have much in common with Audra. Her closet was filled with neat suits and dresses rather than the spandex Audra chose to wear, and the loud music played in clubs hurt Faith's ears. Besides, Faith suspected her neighbor included her in outings only because she'd helped Audra get a job at the insurance company.

"Don't worry," Audra said. "I'll wait while you change."

"Will you be mad if I don't go at all?"

The other woman looked disbelieving. "I don't mind—but why on earth do you want to spend Saturday night at home alone?"

Faith shrugged. "I'm pooped. And I'm thinking about getting up early tomorrow morning." Very early, she thought, a plan forming in her mind.

"You work too much. All you ever do is go to the office or to class or to the library to check out more books."

Faith agreed—sometimes she had mixed feelings about the practical degree she had impoverished herself to obtain. "But tomorrow I'm going to get back to nature. You know, sun and fresh air."

"Doing what?"

"Oh, I thought I'd go out to Rolling Meadows Racecourse to see T.H. The horses work out at daybreak."

"Daybreak?" Audra rolled her eyes. "Okay, whatever turns you on." She flounced away. "I have to get going." But she grinned mischievously when Faith opened the door for her. "Since you're going to so much trouble to see a horse, you might as well introduce yourself to his trainer. What a sexy dude."

Faith didn't admit she also hoped to see Tony up close and personal. Returning to finish the dinner she'd left on the end table, she was shocked to find that Lucy had leapt up and helped herself to most of the chicken chunks.

"You rotten little beast!" she scolded the cat, then laughed. She wasn't hungry anymore. And Lucy was a loving presence in her studio apartment.

Faith glanced around. The place might be small, but she'd done a fairly good job of creating a cozy haven away from the bustle of the city. The walls had been barren and scarred when she'd moved in, so she'd painted them a bright cream and put up colorful if inexpensive posters and prints in plastic frames. She'd chosen sweeping landscapes when-

ever possible, since the only window in the studio looked out
onto a concrete courtyard and brick walls.

She'd also fixed up the used furniture she'd purchased,
sewing a bright slipcover for her nubby brown sofa bed and
refinishing the table, a bookcase and a chest of drawers.
Personal items added the final touch—a cherished quilt
made by her grandmother lay over the back of the sofa, and
above it, on a shelf, sat an old chiming clock that had belonged to her family for generations.

Faith had grown up with that clock, and now she stepped
closer to admire its intricate carved face, then gazed at the
small cluster of framed photographs hanging on either side:
her parents posing before a fence with cornfields and pastures in the background, the old red barn standing on top of
the hill, a teenage Faith smiling as she sat astride a chestnut
quarter horse.

Faith sighed. She hadn't been able to bring Cochise with
her to the city, as she had done with the clock. She still
missed the horse, though she'd lost him thirteen years ago.
He'd played a big role in her old daydreams, sagas in which
she'd been a hero, saved the day and earned the love of a
handsome cowboy.

She guessed her memories and her periodic longings to
live close to nature attracted her to the elemental beauty of
Thoroughbreds and the work of their handlers. So why not
indulge herself and do exactly what she pleased for one
morning? Why not be impetuous for once? She was certainly practical the rest of the time.

Not that a Thoroughbred colt was the same as a sturdy,
hardworking Western steed. And Tony D'Angelo was
nothing like the strong and silent cowboy Faith had once
fancied. She'd read about the Italian-American trainer's
background. He was from New York, and raised in a tough
area of the Bronx. Outspoken, pushy and streetsmart, Tony

had worked his way up from the bottom and had a definite edge, as well as boundless enthusiasm for the horses he trained. He was a sexy dude, all right, if not exactly Faith's type.

The only thing Tony D'Angelo had in common with the cowboy of her dreams was a real fast horse.

"I'll pass," Tony muttered when a waiter came by with a tray of champagne. "If I have any more, I'll fall asleep on my feet. Been up since four this morning."

The waiter nodded and served more appreciative guests nearby. Diamond bracelets glittered as a woman lifted a stem of wine, and a man's laugh rose above the murmur of the crowd packed into the free-flowing, white-on-white living area of the suburban mansion. A string quartet played softly on the landing at the top of an open, winding staircase as a couple in evening clothes descended slowly, pausing to kiss cheeks and shake hands.

Most of the local horse set were present for the posh Saturday-night party, including Tony's bosses, George Langley and Harlan Crandall.

Having seen many similar galas, which he had also been expected to attend, Tony pulled at the collar of his tuxedo shirt and repressed a yawn. He also told himself to be thankful—as a kid, he wouldn't have been allowed on the grounds of this kind of place, much less to rub elbows with its occupants.

Then he saw George Langley heading directly toward him and straightened his posture. Damn! A thickset man with jowls and a permanent scowl, George paid Tony's salary but was often difficult to deal with.

"So how's T.H.?" asked George. "Still favoring his leg?"

"A little. The X rays were clear, but if there's any swelling left tomorrow morning, I'm gonna ship him downstate for a nuclear scan."

"I guess we should be thankful the university has such a progressive veterinary school." George shook his head mournfully. "But, God forbid, if that horse has the smallest hairline crack, we'll have to retire him!"

"Or take him out of racing for a year," agreed Tony. He knew he'd also be bitterly disappointed, but had learned to take his lumps in the unpredictable business of horse racing.

"There go his stud fees, not to mention millions of dollars in purse money." George was a worrywart who always expected the worst. "If only he'd been able to win one more stakes race. What a tragedy!"

"What's this about a tragedy?" intervened Harlan Crandall, who'd approached from another direction.

Great. Now he'd have both of them on his neck, Tony thought dolefully. How many times had he been raked over the coals by owners in the past? How many times had he had to nurse their fragile egos when their horses had failed to do what they wanted?

"T.H. has a hairline crack and won't be able to race anymore," George informed his partner.

"No, it's probably nothing," Tony cut in. "But I can take the horse to Champaign in the morning to make sure."

Harlan raised one eyebrow, but the tall, balding man was easygoing as usual. "Do what you have to, Tony."

"What a tragedy!" George lamented again, making Tony want to strangle him.

"Well, at least we won the Kentucky Derby," Harlan said. "Most people don't even get a chance at it. Do you have someone watching the colt tonight?"

"One of the grooms," Tony told him. "And I thought I'd drop by myself as soon as I can get away from this party."

"Good idea," said Harlan. "Why don't you leave right now?"

Again thankful for the man's reasonable attitude, Tony wasted no time beating a path to the door. Still, there was no peace for the distracted and weary. As he stepped outside and handed his car keys to the parking attendant, he was waylaid by a beautiful redhead in an elegant black dress.

"You're not leaving already, are you, Tony?" asked Margo. She was a sophisticated divorcée who owned horses and was athletic enough to exercise some of them herself. She had a steady boyfriend but always liked to flirt, especially with men who'd been to the winner's circle a lot. "A few of us thought we'd blow this stuffy scene and relax over some drinks at the Bit and Bridle Pub."

"Sorry, no can do, babe."

"Too bad. I didn't even get a chance to dance with you tonight."

Imagining the redhead's lithe limbs pressed against him, Tony ignored his body's quick response.

"Rain check?" he suggested. Margo and her crowd could be a lot of fun, but work responsibilities came first. As a Thoroughbred owner herself, she should understand.

"What's the matter? Got a hot date?"

"It's not a woman—it's a horse."

"A *horse?*" As the attendant drove up with Tony's car, she laughed and bounced away. "No fun, Tony. No wonder your wife divorced you."

Though Margo had only been joking, the remark struck home. Tony brooded about his ex-wife all the way back to Rolling Meadows. Diane had begrudged the time he spent at the barns and the track, but not because she missed being with him. Marrying him when his career was on the rise, she'd been more interested in social climbing than working out a relationship. As soon as she'd gotten a crack at another man with bigger bucks and better connections, she'd wasted no time in changing partners. Had Diane ever loved him at all? Tony wondered bitterly.

He would never know, since people rarely told the truth about their real goals, about how they placed their personal interests above everything else. Sometimes they even lied intentionally, like the trainer's wife who'd gotten him in trouble with her husband and his friends back in New York.

But Tony didn't want to think about that now.

Upon reaching the backstretch of the racecourse, he was waved through by the security guard. He drove down the narrow road between the buildings and parked his low-slung sports car near the barn housing his star colt. Inside, the shedrow was quiet, the horses in the long row of stalls dozing beneath dim lights.

As Tony approached, T.H. stuck his head out over the webbing fronting his stall. Bright-eyed and alert, the chestnut nickered softly.

"How are you, buddy?" Tony affectionately scratched the colt's ears.

Then he ducked under the webbing to check on the problematic leg. Beneath the bandages, the ankle still felt a bit swollen. Better, but Tony didn't want any swelling at all.

"It's off to the vet for you," he muttered as the colt playfully nuzzled Tony's pleated shirtfront, leaving slobber stains on the immaculate white. Tony glanced down at the mess. "Geez, thanks. Now all I need is some manure for after-shave." Ducking back out of the stall, he looked around for the groom he'd told to stay the night. "Pete?" No answer. "Pete!"

Someone grunted, and a human shape detached itself from the shadows. "Yeah, Tony?"

"Did you set up a cot like I told you?" Tony would have stayed himself if he weren't wearing the damned monkey suit.

"It's over there."

"Meantime, put an ice boot on this leg again. I'm going home for a few hours to change my clothes and catch a few Zs. Be back at daybreak."

T.H. was gutsy and genuine, the best horse Tony had ever trained. T.H. had put Tony's name on the map, and Tony intended to see that the colt got the best in return, in both medical attention and career choices. The horse deserved it.

In Tony's book, for openness, courage and pure heart, a horse beat a human being any day of the week.

"You can't go to the backstretch without a license or a special permit, lady," the security guard told Faith when she tried to enter one of the gates leading into the fenced-off area early the next morning.

"Couldn't I sign something? Or leave my driver's license with you? I can be back in fifteen minutes."

"The only place open to the public is the track." The man waved toward Rolling Meadows' tall, elegant grandstand and the racecourse beyond. "That's where the horses are working out."

But not True Heart. Disappointed, Faith turned away. Having arrived a half hour before on the Metra train from downtown, she'd gotten off with a group of backstretch employees arriving for work. Filled with excitement, she'd stood near the fence that bordered the track and watched other horses gallop past, but she hadn't seen the fiery chestnut.

"Drat!" Faith stared at the brightening eastern sky. She'd gotten up at three and taken a long train ride for nothing.

But what could she do? She gazed longingly at the rows of clean-looking white barns beyond the fence, noting a big sign painted on the side of one of the closer buildings: True Heart—Kentucky Derby Winner—Stabled Here.

Faith stopped short and stared. So near and yet so far.

If only she could get a glimpse of the horse. Usually rule-abiding, she found herself wondering if she should try sneaking past the guards. Or climbing over the fence. While she was mulling over the possibilities, she noticed another entrance a few yards down, an open gate that didn't seem to be guarded.

Should she or shouldn't she?

Deciding impetuously that she would, that there might never be another chance, Faith checked around her. Amazingly enough, the coast seemed clear. She slipped inside the fence. One look at the horse couldn't hurt anything. She sped across a lot where several cars and trucks and horse trailers were parked.

She nearly jumped out of her skin when a pickup gunned to a start and began backing up, sending the horse trailer it was towing directly toward her. She dashed out of the vehicle's path and met the glare of its driver, a man with an angular face, freckles and reddish hair. She could see from the narrowing of his beady eyes, he obviously thought it was *her* fault he'd almost hit her. He waved her out of his way, his forearm decorated with a horseshoe tattoo.

At least he didn't tell her she didn't belong on the backstretch.

Turning away, the driver shoved the pickup into gear and rumbled off. Relieved once again, Faith continued on her way, glancing over her shoulder only when she heard the staccato rhythm of hooves pounding on the trailer's walls.

Some unhappy horse was throwing a kicking fit fierce enough to shake the dust off the vehicle's Iowa license plate.

Quickly, Faith approached the barn that bore the big painted sign, taking a deep breath of familiar horse scent and hay as she entered under the cool overhang at the side of the building. She walked down the aisle, past stalls, many of which were empty. A horse whinnied here and there, but, surprisingly enough, there didn't seem to be much activity.

Faith found True Heart's stall near the far end of the long building. Once again disappointed because it was empty, the webbing at the front hanging slack, she almost stumbled over a man lying facedown in the aisle. He groaned.

"Are you all right, mister?" Faith asked with concern. She bent over and touched his shoulder, wincing when she saw the blood on his scalp. "Can I help you?"

"Hey!" growled a voice, gravelly and harsh.

Before she could turn of her own accord, a pair of strong hands took hold of her shoulders and spun her around. She was staring into a pair of familiar dark eyes...and her heart immediately began to speed up.

"What's going on here? Where's my horse?"

Faith could hardly believe she was face-to-face with Tony D'Angelo. He was even better looking, his voice more magnetic, than on television. His large, strong hands encased her upper arms, the contact giving her goose bumps. Overwhelmed by the surprise meeting with the man—and for the moment overlooking his obvious anger—she opened her mouth to answer but didn't get the chance to speak.

"I said, where the hell's my horse?" Tony demanded again, his dark eyes snapping. Then he glanced down at the fallen man. "And what did you do to Pete?"

"I—I..."

Tony shook her until her teeth rattled. "Speak up!"

Coming out of her near trance, Faith grew angry herself. "Stop that!" She pushed at Tony, ignoring the warm, solid flesh beneath the thin shirt he wore. "I didn't do anything to anyone."

Pete rolled over with another groan. "Tony."

His attention switching immediately, Tony finally released Faith, but only to place an iron grip on her upper arm. He dragged her closer to the fallen man.

"They took T.H., Tony," Pete managed to rasp out.

"Who took him?"

Pete rubbed his head. "Don't know. They hit me from behind. Thieves."

Tony turned white. He looked as if he were going to explode. "Somebody stole my horse!"

T.H. had been stolen? Concerned for the horse, but also concerned for the hurt man and for Tony, whom she feared might burst a blood vessel, Faith suggested quietly, "Shouldn't Pete see a doctor?"

Tony let out a deep breath. Some of the color returned to his face. "Right. I'll send him to an emergency room. In the meantime, let me help you," he told Pete, pulling the man to a sitting position with his free hand.

"Thanks, Tony. Just gotta let my head clear."

"Don't try to get up," Tony ordered.

Faith attempted to pry off Tony's fingers from her arm, but he wouldn't let go. In fact, he drew her closer, so close she could smell the coffee on his breath and see the silver strands threading the crisp dark hair at his temples. They hadn't been visible on television. Actually, she'd never imagined she would get *this* close to the man. Even in a fierce, unpleasant mood—understandable, given the circumstances—he exuded a raw, sensual energy that made her heart pound crazily.

Even so, she wished he wouldn't hang on to her so fiercely. "I'm not going anywhere. You can let go."

Tony ignored the complaint. "Who the hell are you, anyway?"

"My name's Faith Murray. I'm visiting."

"Where's your visitor's permit?"

"I don't have one." Uncomfortable, Faith had to tell the truth. "I—I sneaked in here." When Tony scowled, she hurriedly explained. "I just wanted to see True Heart, that's all."

Tony's scowl deepened, the scar above his eyebrow darkening. "Faith Murray?"

"Unfortunately, I didn't see the thieves, either," Faith went on. "When I arrived, Pete was lying on the floor. No one else seemed to be around."

"Faith Murray," Tony repeated the name again, this time with more conviction.

She nodded. "I wish I *had* seen them—I could give a description to the police."

"You're going to be talking to the police, anyway," Tony told her. "I know who you are. You're one of those crazies who wrote the track about setting the horses free."

Faith was surprised. "Setting the horses free?" Was that what Audra had suggested? "I just signed a petition."

"Yeah, I saw your John Henry right at the top of that paper." Tony loomed over her. He was also taller and more intimidating than he looked on television. "What did you do—sneak in here to help some of your animal-rights friends steal my horse?"

Faith's surprise turned to shock. "Of course not!"

Tony noticed Pete stirring, and with his free hand helped the other man struggle to his feet. "Don't hurt yourself, man," he cautioned. "I'll find someone to take you to a hospital." He turned to Faith, his tone menacing. "And as for you, you're gonna stay right here until I come back."

Attempting to ignore his hostility, Faith told herself Tony was only temporarily agitated. "Is there an office where I can sit down?"

"Office? That's too good for a horse thief," he grumbled. "A cell would be more like it."

He actually believed she was a thief! Certain she could straighten things out, however, Faith offered, "Look, I'm willing to talk to the police, but there's no reason I can't make myself comfortable until they get here."

"And give you an opportunity to do a vanishing act?"

His voice no longer held the power to crack her composure. She took a deep breath and tried to get through to him, an edge creeping into her own voice. "I know you're upset, but you're jumping to conclusions. I didn't steal your horse."

For a moment, he gazed at her closely, and she thought he was beginning to understand.

Until he snapped, "You sneaked in here illegally."

"So? That doesn't make me a criminal."

But he was no longer listening. He crossed to True Heart's stall, taking her with him.

"Hey, what are you doing?" she demanded, digging in her heels.

But he easily pulled her inside the enclosure. Her sneakers crunched on the straw that had been the horse's bedding. Tony reached for a leather lunge line hanging nearby.

"I said, what do you think you're doing?" she repeated, her voice rising.

"I'm making certain you don't go anywhere until the police get here."

He quickly twisted the thick cord around her wrists, but seemed careful, as if to make sure it wouldn't hurt her. To no avail, she tried to pull away as Tony fastened her to a hook on the back wall.

"You can't do this!" she cried, furious. And to think she'd believed this man had integrity.

"Watch me. People on the backstretch don't like horse thieves."

"I told you I didn't steal True Heart!"

"Save that for the police."

"I *want* to talk to the police. You can't manhandle someone and tie them up!"

"You can make your claims, lady. I'll make mine. And remember, I've got a lot of friends around here."

Who would all testify against her? Faith wondered worriedly. But she couldn't let Tony just walk away and leave her helpless. "I'll yell and scream if you keep me tied up in this stall!" she threatened.

"Yeah?" Tony looked around and grabbed what looked like a leg bandage, which he tied over Faith's mouth. Again, though, his movements were careful. "People on the backstretch also don't like noise. It bothers the horses."

"Mmmph!"

Faith could only make muted sounds as Tony left her and closed the big double doors of the stall shut behind him. She stared at the blank, windowless walls.

What irony.

Feeling boxed in by her schedule, her budget, her small apartment, Faith had come to the racetrack to soak up some fresh air and freedom by watching True Heart run.

Instead, she was a prisoner in his stall!

Feeling a twinge of remorse as he helped Pete out of the barn, Tony paused to glance over his shoulder at the closed stall. Either Faith Murray was telling the truth or she was putting on a damned good act. How could anyone suspect such a clean-cut, pretty young woman of being a thief? Especially after gazing into her big, innocent-looking blue eyes.

Those eyes had tugged at him, had threatened to touch his heart—something he was unwilling to let any woman do again.

But even if she wasn't the actual thief, Faith could have been a decoy, Tony assured himself, turning away. He couldn't let a gorgeous set of baby blues sway him. Trust was for fools. Other women had used him and fooled him and, with T.H. missing, he couldn't take any chances.

Chapter Two

Faith's outrage cooled by the time Tony returned a half hour later. He didn't say much, but his manner seemed softer as he untied her and escorted her to the other end of the building to talk to the police. Prone to making excuses for people, she remembered watching a television bio about him—he'd had a very hard life. He was used to being tough and was very upset over his missing horse.

But now, obviously having realized he'd made a mistake, he would surely apologize, she thought.

No such luck.

She became upset all over again when the police acted friendly toward the trainer and distinctly suspicious and threatening toward her. They asked her over and over how it was she'd happened to sneak onto the backstretch on the very morning a valuable racehorse was stolen. Unused to such scrutiny by the authorities, Faith got so uptight, she forgot about making any counterclaims herself.

"We're going to be keeping an eye on you, Miss Murray," one detective warned her as he and his tight-lipped companions left the barn.

She nodded, wishing she'd never come out to Rolling Meadows in the first place. Good grief, she'd never so much as received a traffic ticket before, and now she was a suspect in an incident involving grand theft and battery.

"I'm gonna be keeping an eye on you, too," Tony muttered.

Arms crossed, expression cool, he'd been standing right beside her during the interview. All he'd told the police was that he'd found her standing over an unconscious Pete.

"What do you mean you're going to be keeping an eye on me?" she asked as he escorted her out of the barn, hand at her elbow. Since his grip was gentle if firm, she allowed it...and tried to ignore the tingling sensation rippling up her arm.

"I haven't forgotten that petition you signed."

She'd wondered why he hadn't mentioned it to the authorities.

"But I like to play my own hand," he went on in explanation. "A smart man keeps a few cards to himself. I still have something on you."

Disappointed that he refused to believe her, Faith hardened her jaw and her heart. "Well, both you and the police can watch me all you like. You'll soon find out I had nothing to do with the kidnapping. Like I've been saying all along, I'm not guilty." And she wouldn't feel sorry for him!

Tony responded coolly, "Look, I just want my horse back." Then an odd look crossed his face—pain? "T.H. is the greatest, in both the talent and temperament departments. I have to get him back. He doesn't deserve..." He clammed up and glared as he realized Faith was watching him closely.

At least he cared about True Heart. But Faith nevertheless was hurt and insulted that he thought her culpable. "You must not have very good judgment where people are concerned, or you would know I'm no criminal."

"I'm not psychic."

Upset that the horse was missing, unnerved that she was under suspicion and disappointed that she had misjudged Tony, Faith was relieved to sight the gate she'd so stupidly entered without permission. Now she couldn't wait to beat a hasty retreat.

But when she tried to pull away, Tony tightened his hold. "Where do you think you're going?"

"Home. Where I can forget about this mess."

"I don't think so."

She caught her breath in alarm. "What do you mean, you don't think so? Look, I already talked to the police. Are you going to call them back and ask them to put me in jail?"

"I told you I like to play my own hand." He hesitated, then said, "I'm taking you into personal custody."

"Personal what?"

"You're sticking close to me, Faith Murray—at least until I find out what happened to my horse."

He couldn't be serious! "I told you I don't know where True Heart is. I don't have any—"

"Save it." He cut her off with a wave. "I've heard your excuses already." He took hold of her shoulders and pointed her toward a black sports car parked nearby. "We're going for a little ride."

Once again, Faith was outraged. But the fact that he wasn't handling her roughly gave her confidence. Tony D'Angelo might be disagreeable, but she didn't think he was dangerous.

"You can't order me around. I don't want to go with you and I don't have to!"

"Get in." Tony opened the passenger door.

"You can't force me against my will." She glanced around wildly, hoping someone would notice the situation. But the man leading a horse past them a few yards away didn't even glance in their direction. She raised her voice. "You can't kidnap me!"

"I don't plan to hold you for ransom."

"You can't hold me at all. I'm going to call the police myself if you even try."

He leaned closer, his dark eyes opaque and threatening. "Go ahead. Then I'll press charges and show them that petition. I'll tell them I found out you're a member of a radical animal-rights group and they'll put you in jail. You'd better know somebody with plenty of bail money."

Was the petition and trespassing on the backstretch enough incriminating evidence? Faith wondered. She knew little about criminal law or police procedure, but with his reputation and his money connections via True Heart's owners, Tony definitely had more clout than she did. She would feel terrible if she had to call her financially strapped parents and ask them to bail her out of jail.

Not to mention humiliated.

"Are you gonna get in or not?"

Swallowing tightly, Faith finally obeyed. Given time, maybe she could talk some sense into Tony. He might be tough and, at the moment, desperate beneath his hard facade, but surely he had a heart.

The trainer got in the other side of the car and drove.

Faith nearly felt like crying. What a horrible situation! But Tony might sneer if she broke down in front of him. So she blinked back the trace of moisture in her eyes and took a deep breath. She couldn't believe she'd actually been so excited about finally seeing the man up close and personal.

Well, this was far too close and definitely too personal for her taste!

When she was finally able to focus on her surroundings, a suburban highway, she asked tightly, "Where are we going?"

"To my house."

"Am I allowed to ask why?"

"I want to make a few calls."

"You couldn't do that at the barns?"

"I need more privacy." He paused. "I also want a more private talk with you. I want to know all about you, about everyone you know."

Wonderful, Faith thought, hoping Tony wouldn't sic the police on Audra. Her friend was the only person she knew who had anything to do with animal activists.

If animal activists had kidnapped True Heart, which she doubted.

A few more miles down the road, Faith's captor pulled his car into an attractive town-house complex. Tony's place looked exactly like its neighbors, a neat brick two-story with a sloping slate roof and gray-trimmed windows and doors. Unlike most of the other houses, though, Tony's had no flower beds out front, nor any hanging plants on the small porch at the building's entrance.

Inside, the house was even more stark, a study in contrast to her own homey apartment. Thick, luxurious shag carpeted the combination dining and living room, but the only furniture was an expensive leather chair, a desk, a long, striped couch, an end table and a television. A crumpled blanket and pillow lay on the couch, making it appear as if Tony had slept there the night before. Why hadn't he used one of the upstairs bedrooms? Were they barren, perhaps? Maybe Tony had only a few pieces of furniture.

And not many personal objects, either. No pictures hung on the walls, no treasured possessions sat amid the papers piled on the desk built into one wall. In Tony's house, the only indication of his personality and interests were copies of *The Blood-Horse* magazine and several framed photos on the end table of racehorses receiving prizes in the winner's circle.

Faith couldn't help wondering why anyone would want to spend so much money on a town house and not fix it up. The place had so many possibilities, so much room. She wished she had *half* this much space.

As soon as he locked the dead bolt on the front door, Tony let go of Faith and pointed at the couch. "Sit."

"Want me to roll over and play dead, too?" she snapped sarcastically as she plopped down.

"Don't be cute."

Her anger flared. "I'll be cute if I want to."

Tony glared. "I don't like mouthy women."

She raised her chin. "Well, I don't like *you*. You're an insufferable creep."

Oops. Now it would be even more difficult to talk sense into the trainer. Not that Tony didn't deserve her hostility. She'd just about had enough of this situation. Too bad she hadn't confined her admiration for True Heart to the comfort of watching him on videotape from her seat on the couch. So much for impetuosity!

Tony rifled through the papers on his desk. "Save the name-calling. You aren't that good at it—I've been called a lot worse."

"I can understand why. You'd better be nicer to horses than you are to human beings, or I might actually *join* an animal activist group and persecute you."

He didn't seem worried by the threat; instead he scowled at an address book he'd pulled off his desk. "Don't worry, I'm much nicer to horses."

And he probably was.

Musing about when she'd get a chance to make a run for it and find her way back to the city, Faith watched as Tony sat on the desk and made a quick phone call, listening to his gravelly, husky, sexy voice. Even now, when she was so angry, she had to admit Tony was more attractive in person than he'd been on television. She admired his lean grace despite herself. His shoulders were wide enough to fill out his striped shirt and casual jacket, while his khaki pants revealed a trim waist and flat belly. He kept himself in nearly as good shape as his horses.

Distracted, she forced herself to focus on the telephone conversation. Tony seemed to be talking to an assistant trainer, someone he asked to take charge for a few days while he dealt with the missing T.H.

A few days? Faith was startled. But surely Tony wouldn't keep her captive for that long. She was due in to work tomorrow. Well, she decided, she'd simply put up a screaming fit if he even dared try to hold her beyond the next couple of hours. Surely the police wouldn't really arrest her.

She examined Tony closely as he replaced the receiver and punched in another number. Once a tough kid, he'd probably gotten that scar and crooked nose in a fight. No doubt he'd also built up his cynical attitude toward people on the mean streets, too.

Tony noticed her scrutiny. "What are you staring at?"

"Who broke your nose?"

"A guy who looked a lot worse when I got through with him."

She should have expected a macho answer.

Tony switched his attention to the phone. "George? This is Tony. Uh...you what?" Tony's brows rose, then his voice. "An anonymous call? My God, if they harm him I'll..."

Faith couldn't help but respond to the rising tension. Harm True Heart? She rose and moved toward the desk, though she tried to appear casual as she leaned in closer to the receiver and strained to hear. She also tried to ignore the way her body reacted to being so close to the trainer.

"They can't get away with this!" Tony's expression made him appear dangerous. But as he continued to listen, he settled down a bit. "I'll— Yeah, I guess that's a good idea. I already talked to the police."

She leaned close enough to hear a booming voice coming through the loosely held receiver.

"What about Pete?" she heard the owner demand. "Did he see anything?"

"Nah, they knocked him for a loop, but I'm going back to the track to ask some questions."

"I'm going to call Harlan again. Couldn't get hold of him before. I knew things were going too good! I knew we were in for a disaster of some sort."

Tony made a disgusted face. "We'll do whatever's necessary to get T.H. back. Talk to you later."

Then he hung up, whipped around and practically came nose to nose with Faith. Startled by the close proximity, surprised by the electricity zinging along her nerve endings, she backed off immediately. Despite the tense, negative situation, she found being near Tony more exciting than she'd have liked it to be.

"So what happened?" Faith knew she was blushing and hoped he didn't notice. "Are the kidnappers threatening to hurt True Heart?"

"They're gonna kill him unless they get two million in cash."

Her heart sank. "Kill him! Oh, no!" She pictured the horse surging down the track, his tail flying behind him like a banner. "How could anyone hurt an innocent animal?"

"I don't know." Tony gazed at her assessingly. "Maybe they aren't animal activists, after all."

"Of course not. Anybody with any sense would've known that from the very beginning. That was just *your* crazy idea."

He continued to stare at her.

"We have to do something," she went on.

"We?"

She reworded the generality. "Er, I mean, you. You have to do something."

He nodded. "I agree. And I'm going to take action with or without the police." Once again, he took hold of her shoulders, then turned her toward the couch. "But first we're gonna have that little talk."

"Unbelievable. You still want to question me? You're wasting time."

"I'll make it short and to the point."

"I don't know anything!"

"So you keep saying." He pointed at the couch. "Sit."

This time Faith didn't object. Her worry for the horse was greater than her aggravation with Tony, who was sounding less and less mean. How could thieves be so cruel and greedy as to harm such a beautiful animal? She identified with True Heart and couldn't help but take such a threat personally.

After talking to Faith Murray for a while, Tony still had to admit she sounded as if she were telling the truth. He had forced himself to be hard on her because of his concern for T.H., who was already in double trouble, due to the injury. If anything happened to that horse... Just thinking about it tied his gut in knots.

Now, looking at Faith, he felt another twinge of guilt about treating her with so little respect. He only hoped he hadn't bruised her, dragging her around as he had. He tried reminding himself he had good reasons for not believing anyone. He was used to dealing with people who had ulterior motives—handicappers and sportswriters who wanted tips, rivals who had big chips on their shoulders, giddy women who liked to attach themselves to top trainers as some kind of status symbol, other people who hoped to use him for his connections or to soak up some of the limelight they thought he basked in.

Somebody was always out for something.

Though Faith actually seemed for real. Even her associates were ordinary folk, people she worked with or shared night-school classes with. The only person who seemed remotely suspicious in any way was her flaky neighbor Audra.

What impressed Tony most about Faith was that she also cared about his horse. Or else she was putting on the best damned act he'd ever seen.

He leaned back in his seat beside her on the couch. "God, you're a regular Mary Poppins."

A tiny line appeared between the soft wings of her eyebrows. "Mary Poppins? What do you mean by that?"

"All sweet and innocent and wide-eyed." And very, very pretty. Not that her looks affected his judgment.

She assumed what was probably meant to be a scowl. "I believe Mary Poppins was a witch or some such, so don't be fooled."

Undeterred by the threat, Tony found himself just a little amused . . . and wanting to know more about her. "Are you really twenty-eight?"

"Do you want to see my driver's license?"

"Okay. Might as well check out the statistics."

LOVE ON THE RUN

She rolled her eyes heavenward and fished in her purse for the document.

He examined the license when she handed it over. "Yeah, twenty-eight, unless this is forged."

She gave an exasperated sigh. "Do you ever believe anything anyone tells you?"

"It's just that you're so...uh, wholesome looking," he muttered, giving her another quick once-over and ignoring the warmth spreading through him as he did. He would be a real sucker to fall for this cutie and then find she had some connection to the crime. "I could believe you were even younger. Maybe it's that clean, clear complexion and those big baby blues."

"My eyes are blue-gray—like the license says."

But he didn't look at the license. "Okay, blue-gray." Now that he'd calmed down some, he couldn't help but inspect her more personally.

Her wavy light-brown hair, which she wore in a chin-length bob, looked as if it would be silk to the touch and smelled like the fresh outdoors. He was close enough to tell. Wouldn't mind getting even closer. His gaze swept over her straight nose, her pretty mouth that turned up at the corners, then moved lower. Beneath the blue sweatshirt and jeans, Faith had a nicely rounded figure.

Obviously realizing he was evaluating her, she snatched the driver's license back from him and glared. "I'll put this away, if you don't mind."

Tony repressed a smile. Faith Murray might be innocent looking, but she had spirit. He liked that in a woman, just as he did in his horses.

"Where did you say you came from?" he asked.

"Where was I born? Iowa."

"Farm country."

"I was raised on a farm, true."

That's where she'd gotten the fresh, healthy look. "Why did you come to the city?"

"To get a job."

Oh, yeah, she'd already said that. "And where did you say you worked?"

"Pilgrim Insurance Company."

He glanced at her pink, perfectly shaped lips again, and couldn't stop himself from asking, "Do you have a boyfriend?"

"I haven't dated for awhile."

No one had been kissing that pretty mouth? "Why not?" he asked, tempted to volunteer.

She turned her big eyes on him. "I haven't had time."

"Nobody broke your heart or anything?" His heart was racing with his fantasies.

She shook her head again.

"Have you ever been serious about anyone?" he inquired, realizing that he really was drawn to her. Unusual. Faith Murray certainly wasn't his type.

She drew back slightly and gave him a suspicious scowl. "Does this line of questioning have anything to do with your missing horse?"

Suddenly realizing he'd revealed his interest despite his intentions, Tony covered. "I just want to know your connections. Maybe you dated a criminal one time."

"I don't date criminals," she pointed out. "What about your own connections? It makes more sense that somebody you know took your horse or knows something about him. There must be plenty of shady characters at the track."

"Hey," he objected, "a person isn't sleazy just because he works at the track. I started out as a hot-walker myself." He'd cooled horses for more than a year until he became an assistant groom. "And nobody's allowed on the backstretch without a license."

"That doesn't mean they wouldn't steal."

"No," he admitted. And it wasn't as if the backstretch was real stable. Many employees were like gypsies, traveling from track to track. "I'm gonna question people, ask them if they saw a horse trailer this morning."

"A trailer?"

"They had to load T.H. onto something. And it takes at least two men to get him to go up a ramp."

"A trailer," she repeated, looking thoughtful. "I saw a pickup and trailer pulling away right before I came into your barn."

Tony seized upon that information. "What kind of pickup?"

"I'm not sure of the make, but it was dark blue and beat-up. The driver almost ran me over."

"Did you see him up close?"

"He had an angular face with freckles and reddish hair."

Tony thought hard, but the description didn't ring a bell.

"Could he have been stealing True Heart?" Faith asked. "I didn't even remember the trailer until now."

"Any lead is worth following up. What else do you remember about this guy? Was he big? Small? Young or old?"

"I couldn't tell about his build, but he was middle-aged, I guess."

"Was anyone with him?"

"I think so, but I couldn't see. The trailer had an Iowa license plate, I remember that."

"That could be a lead. Someone else had to have seen it. We have to go back to the track."

We.

Tony noticed Faith didn't object to the term, and when he rose to get ready to go, so did she.

Maybe she was for real, someone who sincerely cared about the fate of his horse. Perhaps she'd been telling the truth when she'd claimed she'd only sneaked into the back-stretch to get a look at T.H.

But even so, Tony told himself to be careful. No matter how innocent Faith seemed, he couldn't let himself trust her so easily. After years of taking care of problems by himself, he knew better.

They were walking across the backstretch at Rolling Meadows when Faith realized things had changed. Tony hadn't made any threats on the drive back, not even to get her in or out of the car. He must have finally accepted her story, she thought with satisfaction. Of course, she also wondered if she shouldn't leave now while she had the chance.

She would, she supposed, if she didn't feel so badly about T.H. . . . and if she weren't so fascinated by the unusual situation, which was an adventure of sorts. It had nothing to do with Tony D'Angelo, she assured herself.

Her thoughts returned to worry for the horse as they walked through a barn. "Are the owners going to pay True Heart's ransom?"

"They'd better come up with the money. That's the best colt—and the biggest money-maker—they'll ever get."

"If they can afford it, why don't they simply pay the ransom?" She wished True Heart meant more than money to these men, but she wouldn't fool herself. Racehorses were probably just investments and status symbols to them. "Wouldn't that be easier than conducting your own investigation?"

"Kidnappers don't necessarily keep promises. I like to hedge my bets."

In other words, play his own cards, Faith thought, un-
surprised. "If you find out anything important," she asked,
"are you going to tell the police?"

"Maybe, maybe not."

"You might not? Don't you believe they'd try to help?"

"I learned a long time ago to depend on myself."

"How long?"

"Oh, twenty years or so. I've been on my own since I was
sixteen."

Sixteen? Taken aback—and to her dismay, almost feeling as much compassion for him as she did for the horse—
Faith murmured, "You ran away from home?"

He frowned. "That's enough with the questions."

Though he'd asked plenty of her. Of course, he was a defensive and distrustful person, which no doubt accounted
for his earlier treatment of her. Not that the knowledge
made his initial behavior okay.

She saw that Tony could be sociable when he wanted. As
he questioned grooms, trainers, assistant trainers, hot-
walkers, exercise riders and jockeys, he seemed to know how
to handle each in a firm yet personable manner. At the same
time, he made no attempt to introduce Faith, and she knew
the trainer's acquaintances were wondering who in the heck
she was.

One man wearing battered Western boots and a purple
cap smiled at Faith as he asked directly, "Who's this?"

Tony glanced at his companion, as if he'd forgotten she'd
been following him around. He raised one brow, offering
quickly, "This is my girlfriend." And he slung an arm
around Faith's shoulders, surprising her even more. She
opened her mouth to say something, only to have Tony take
hold of her chin, stopping her from protesting. "She's such
a cutie."

A cutie? Faith could see from the expression on his face that he wanted her to go along with him. But she couldn't help but stiffen as he pressed her closer to his lean, hard body. He surely couldn't expect her to act all lovey-dovey after the way he'd treated her.

"Don't be shy, babe."

"Shy?" squeaked Faith, the only word she got out before Tony covered her mouth with a quick, smacking kiss that left her speechless . . . and her pulse racing.

The man in the purple cap widened his eyes. "Wow, you must be serious, Tony. Never seen you parade a woman around the backstretch before."

Her face burning, her lips tingling, Faith again tried to move away from Tony. She couldn't believe the way she was responding to him after all he'd put her through in the last couple of hours!

"Don't worry," she told the man. "I don't care—"

"She doesn't care what I did in the past," Tony interrupted swiftly. "You know, playing the field and all. Faith is a little gem." This time he brushed his warm lips across her forehead. "Aren't you, babe?"

Her forehead seared by the contact, Faith scowled. Babe? Did Tony think that was a term of endearment? And what did he mean by playing the field? How many women did he usually date? Even more upsetting, why should she care?

Before she could protest, he was already pulling her toward one of the barns. "Well, thanks, Sam. I'd appreciate your telling me anything you hear."

"Sure thing, Tony," said the other man, watching them leave, his expression curious.

As soon as they got inside the shady overhang of the barn, Tony let Faith jerk away.

She whirled toward him. "And just what did you think you were doing out there?"

"Pretending you're my girlfriend."

"And why is that? Why couldn't you tell that man the truth?"

"You'd rather he knew you're under suspicion of grand theft? That I have you in custody?"

She caught her breath, stunned. "I thought you'd gotten over that ridiculous idea." She'd thought he'd believed her. "I came to the track with you because I wanted to. You didn't force me."

"I would have if I'd had to."

But the conviction he'd had earlier was missing, Faith noticed. "You said animal-rights activists couldn't have done the kidnapping," she pointed out. "So why detain me?"

"I don't know who's responsible." He took hold of her arm and marched her down the aisle past the stalls. "But either you stay with me until I do or I turn you over to the cops. Sorry, but you need to cooperate."

Sorry. He'd actually said the word.

"If I could get T.H. back, believe me, I would," she insisted. "I only wish I could help. But I have to go to work tomorrow. You can't keep me longer than today."

"You might have to call in sick. I need—" He cut off the last sentence.

He needed what? Her? Why?

Faith's emotions were awhirl as Tony stopped to talk to a couple of men who were bathing a horse, watering down the suds with a garden hose. Despite her mental state, she noted Tony's posture—his feet planted wide, his shoulders back. He had the arrogant bearing of a confident male. He had an

arrogant walk, too, she'd noticed, a touch of the strut he'd
probably picked up on the streets of New York.

Yet he was far more vulnerable than he let on. The edge
to his voice, the nervous way he kept his hands shoved in his
pockets, showed he really cared about his horse...if one was
sensitive enough to pick up on it. And it seemed nobody
was. No one but her. Everyone answered his questions, but
no one volunteered to do anything more than keep their eyes
and ears open.

That didn't seem exactly supportive. Though she was only
a fan, if and when the horse could be located, Faith knew
she would willingly face danger to rescue T.H. Fervor
building, she swore to herself she would swim a raging river,
run into a burning building, maybe even dodge bullets. She
felt a lump in her throat every time she thought about the
beautiful animal being used by some greedy criminals. The
horse had already won against great odds; now someone was
trying to take his life away for their own selfish purposes.
That made her see red. She truly and deeply cared.

Could that be why Tony wanted her around...because he
sensed the depth of her concern and so he wouldn't feel so
alone? She looked at him in a new light, wondering why he
couldn't be honest about it, instead of using threats to keep
her with him.

When he finished with the men, he circled her back with
his arm. "Come on, babe."

She walked beside him, but she couldn't help lashing out,
"Do you call all your girlfriends 'babe'?"

"What's the matter with that?"

"It sounds awful, very unromantic."

"Nobody ever complained about my romantic ability."

She knew he was referring to physical romance, not emotional. "Maybe they didn't have time to complain, since

you've dated so many of them. What do they get—one night apiece?''

He stared down his nose. ''One night, two nights . . . as long as it takes to keep up my reputation.''

''I'm sure you have a reputation, all right,'' she mumbled.

''Are you trying to insult me?''

Boy, was he insecure. ''Who, me? Miss Mary Poppins?''

Knowing she'd finally gotten his goat, that she had his number, Faith hid her smirk by glancing to the side. A pop machine stood near one of the jockey dormitories.

Her mouth had been dry for quite some time. ''I'd like a can of cola.''

''Okay, but make it fast.''

''Fast to drink it or fast to get the can out of the machine?''

''Both.''

What a turkey, Faith thought, wondering what he'd do when she needed to stop at a rest room.

They headed for the backstretch office where Tony inquired about shipments of horses, arrivals and departures. Faith glanced about. If nothing else, she was getting an insider's tour of the track.

''There weren't supposed to be any arrivals or departures today that I know of,'' the man in the office told Tony. ''I heard about your trouble. We're doing everything we can. We'll keep our eyes and ears open.''

The same old phrase.

But Tony nodded. ''Thanks.''

On their way out of the office, they met a fashionably dressed redheaded woman who really gave Faith the once-over.

Though his face showed no emotion, Faith could tell Tony was a bit taken aback. "Hi, Margo."

The redhead smiled. "You had to see a horse last night, hmm, Tony?"

"Yeah, I did."

"A pretty little filly, I bet. No wonder you didn't have time to go out for a drink."

Faith took a sip of cola and glanced from Tony to Margo. One of his conquests? She realized she might have the trainer in a very messy situation.

"What's your name?" Margo asked Faith.

Faith only hesitated for a moment. "Babe." Tony stiffened, but she didn't care. "It's his personal nickname for me," she told Margo.

To her credit, the redhead grinned. "He seems to have that nickname for a lot of people."

"But he only says it in his special way to me," Faith assured the other woman, reveling in making Tony as uncomfortable as he had made her. Turnabout was only fair play. "Not that I care about getting serious or anything. It's only physical—he's got such stamina."

Margo raised her brows.

"Okay, okay," Tony cut in, obviously wanting out of the situation. His grip tightened on Faith as he practically dragged her away. "We've got to get going." They headed back toward the barns. "Think you're real funny, don't you?"

"You deserve to be made fun of."

"I didn't know you had such a mouth on you."

"I guess you bring out my best."

"And you're a helluva lot more sophisticated than you let on."

"I never claimed to be innocent, just honest . . . babe."

He stopped short, appearing really put out. "Quit jerking me around or I'll put a muzzle on you."

"Ha! I'd like to see you explain *that* to your backstretch friends."

"Then I guess I'll have to shut you up some other way."

Faith dropped the soda can as Tony pulled her tightly against him and covered her mouth with a searching kiss.

"Mmmph," she objected half-heartedly before closing her eyes and slowly winding her arms around his neck.

Meeting the real Tony may have reduced her respect for him but, unfortunately, it hadn't blunted his physical appeal one bit.

Chapter Three

Faith was overwhelmed by the intensity of the moment as Tony molded her against him, deepening the kiss. His tongue invaded, conquering hers with a jolt of heat that awoke something dwelling in her most secret spaces.

Their breaths melded, their heartbeats blended. Faith wasn't sure whose pulse was racing at such a shuddering pace, his or hers. The pressure of his hands on her body was exquisite, especially when he lifted the back of her sweatshirt and slid a callused palm over her bare skin. Her knees went weak.

"Hr-r-mph."

Tony raised his head, and Faith opened her eyes.

They were being observed.

As she struggled to make Tony release her, an older guy wearing a sports coat and a battered felt hat had the decency to turn his head.

"Tony," Faith whispered through gritted teeth, "we're not alone. Let go!"

When he did, she blushed and tried to look nonchalant as she struggled to get her pulse and breathing under control. She couldn't believe she'd allowed herself even that one moment of madness, not after all Tony had put her through.

She didn't want to admit a teeny, tiny part of her heart was still racing with excitement.

To her chagrin, Tony didn't appear moved at all as he said, "Afternoon, Stan."

"Tony."

The men shook hands. Stan Berg was an old-time, well-known horse trainer Faith recognized from the Kentucky Derby videotape. Stan's colt Scandalous had run in the famous race. His eyes twinkled as he gave Faith an interested once-over, winked broadly, then turned back to Tony.

"Uh, sorry to disturb you lovebirds, but I heard you were inquiring about a suspicious-looking character that might have been involved with True Heart's disappearance."

Tony drew himself together and, as if finally realizing he'd let himself forget about T.H. for a moment, tensed. "Yeah. A skinny, freckled guy with reddish hair."

"A coupla weeks ago I fired a groom who fit that description. Name's Zak Hobson. A real surly cuss, but good with horses. Couldn't keep him after he pulled a knife and threatened one of my other employees."

"Zak Hobson." Tony repeated the name thoughtfully. "I suppose you wouldn't know what happened to him afterward? Where he went?"

"One of my other grooms said Zak was heading for Kentucky to get another job," Stan said. "Why don't you call one of the boys down there and ask about him? Tell them he has a big tattoo on one arm."

Faith immediately connected with the information. "Tattoo?" She visualized the man who'd nearly run her over her. "A horseshoe?"

Stan fastened his gaze on her once again. "That's right, little lady."

"Then I'm certain this Zak guy was the man in the pickup," she said excitedly. "I saw the tattoo on his forearm."

Tony frowned. "And you're just telling me this now?"

Did he have to be suspicious even when she was trying to help? "I didn't remember until now." He'd had her too angry and scared with his inquisition act. "My mind was on other things at the time."

"Like sneaking into my barn."

"What's this?" Stan asked, his curiosity obviously aroused.

Getting a handle on his irritation, Tony placed a proprietary hand on Faith's shoulder. "You know how women can be. She was desperate to see me this morning."

Stan merely grunted, no doubt aware of Tony's lover-boy reputation.

"I'm desperate all right," Faith said sarcastically, trying to push his hand off her shoulder. The warm weight of his fingers was making her pulse quicken again, and she told herself she wanted nothing more to do with the man.

But Tony merely took hold of her objecting hand and gave it a warning squeeze. "Calling the tracks in Kentucky would be a waste of time," he mused. "Even if Hobson got a job somewhere, he was obviously in Illinois this morning."

"The trailer had an Iowa license plate," Faith pointed out, certain she could remember the number if she concentrated.

"Wait a minute," Stan said, his forehead wrinkling. "Hobson talked about having people in Iowa."

"Where in Iowa?" Tony asked.

"Don't know for sure. Sorry I can't be of more help."

"You've been a big enough help already," Tony said. "Thanks for the information, Stan."

"I'll let you know if I remember anything else. Damn horse thieves," the old trainer grumbled as he passed them.

Faith squeezed her eyes shut and envisioned the scene that morning. The driver waving her off... the sound of the horse's hooves... the glimpse she got of the dusty license plate.

"Dubuque County," she said. "The county is listed across the bottom of Iowa plates."

"What about the number?"

"SVA and 2 something." She closed her eyes again, but the other two numbers wouldn't gel. "I'm not sure. Maybe if I—"

"You really think you'll remember?"

"Could be. I grew up beside a highway and one of my childhood games was to lie on a hill and see if I could read a license plate before a car passed by."

"Not much to do in Iowa, huh?" Tony observed.

Faith wondered if he was making fun of her, but his mind seemed to be strictly on business once more.

"Remembering the county—that's a sign," he was muttering to himself, his tone intense. "The town of Dubuque is only a few hours drive from here. That's where Hobson took T.H. Yeah, I'd stake my life's savings on Dubuque County."

"*If* Zak Hobson actually went to Iowa at all. It would be easy to hide a horse in Indiana or Wisconsin—even downstate Illinois."

"Then why bring a trailer from Dubuque? It musta come off a farm where they planned to stash the colt. At least, that's what my gut tells me. I haven't had such a strong hunch since the first time I saw T.H. run. I knew I had a winner—and my buddy came through for me. I can't let him down. I gotta find him before he gets hurt."

Tony was talking to himself. He was preoccupied, almost as if he'd forgotten about her presence. Staring at the worried frown creasing his brow, Faith was empathetic. He was hurting, just as Faith would be if something happened to her beloved Lucy. At least for him, getting T.H. back wasn't a matter of dollars and cents.

Beneath that tough, calculating exterior beat the heart of a real human being, no matter how hard he tried to hide it.

Intent on following up their only lead before it got cold, Tony wanted to take off for Dubuque right then and there, but figured he had to confer with T.H.'s owners first.

"Let's get a move on." He automatically took Faith's arm and was relieved when she didn't resist.

"Now where to?"

"Green Meadows Farm in Barrington. George and Amelia Langley's place."

When she didn't argue, Tony gave Faith a searching look and was surprised by her open expression. As their eyes connected, he felt the air zinging between them and, for once, without hostility. The kiss had done it, he thought. Surprised him. Changed things. Rang his chimes in rock 'n' roll time. He only hoped that the physical attraction and the more puzzling feeling beneath it didn't mean he'd gotten himself into something he was going to be sorry about in the future.

Still holding on to her, his stride long and hurried, he made for his car. He slowed only when he realized Faith had to jog to keep up with him. Her face was flushed, her big eyes bright, her lips parted as she breathed a little too quickly.

And his own pulse quickened in response.

God, how he wanted to kiss her again, to explore the smooth, warm skin beneath her sweatshirt. But if he continued to fantasize about doing so, he wouldn't be able to keep his mind on business. And on the fact that he still had reason to suspect her. No human could possibly be as genuine and as pure of heart as Faith Murray appeared. He'd had too much life experience to believe that.

And yet, part of him wanted to believe in her, one hundred percent . . . part of him wanted to believe in *someone*.

He was thoughtful and silent until they were settled in the Porsche and traveling on Northwest Highway toward Barrington. "So why the big fascination with horses?" he finally asked. Maybe he could get her to spill some truth that would either justify or nix his overly suspicious nature.

"I'm a farm girl, remember. I learned to ride practically before I was walking. What about you?"

"My dad had a thing for the ponies." His real father—not the crud his mother had mistakenly married several years after being widowed. "Playing them, that is. He took me to the track practically before I was walking."

He echoed her and made a joke of it because he didn't want to talk about the events that had led up to his becoming a trainer. Even now, the past was still vivid and painful. Very few people knew the whole truth about him, and he intended to keep it that way.

He turned the conversation back on her. "So you had your own horse on the farm?"

"Cochise. He was a chestnut quarter horse." Her voice tightened a little. "When I watched the Kentucky Derby on television, True Heart reminded me of him. Part of the reason I'm such a fan."

"Yeah. My good buddy isn't the typical-looking Thoroughbred, is he?" he admitted. "But even if T.H. doesn't have the size and lines of his ancestors, he does have the heart, and that's what counts." His throat tightened. "Heart's the most important thing a trainer can hope for."

When Faith remained silent, he gave her a quick glance and realized she was staring at him, her own expression thoughtful, almost as if she were seeing him with new eyes. As if she'd found something to like about him.

Tightening his jaw and hardening himself against the unusual emotions she stirred up in him, he looked away and concentrated on the road until they approached Green Meadows Farm, which lay several miles west of the town of Barrington. This corner of Illinois always amazed him with its rolling, white-fenced pastures and canopies of trees, reminding him of Kentucky bluegrass country.

"Oh, how beautiful," Faith murmured.

Sneaking a sideways peak at her, Tony thought *she* was beautiful. A big smile wreathed her face, and her eyes shone as she eagerly observed pastured mares and half-grown foals. And her eyebrows shot up in awe when she got a glimpse of the Country French estate house sprawled on a hill overlooking the fields.

With satisfaction, he noted George's BMW among the several cars parked in the circular drive. He pulled over and cut the engine.

As Tony expected, the house was in an uproar. The front door stood wide open, and he and Faith entered unnoticed. In the sunken living room to the right, several people were discussing the kidnapping situation as a manservant passed out drinks. A uniformed maid flew by from one side of the house to the other. Glimpsing the two newcomers standing in the doorway, she skidded to a halt.

"Mr. Langley will be out in a few minutes," she said.

"I think he'll want to see me right now."

"The family room—" the harried-looking maid pointed "—to your left and down the stairs."

"They should hand out maps of a place this size at the door," Faith whispered as they crossed the foyer. "This hall is as big as my whole apartment."

Tony stopped her from going farther when George's voice rang out loud and clear from the lower level.

"This isn't the time to bring up spending that kind of money, Amelia!"

"But I want my own Florida house," his wife complained. "We're there every winter during Gulfstream's season. It's humiliating to have to depend on friends for a place to stay."

"I told you we can rent a house."

"Not one up to our standards, George."

"You have two nice homes—this one and the condo on Lake Michigan. We can't afford a third," George stated. "The economy is sour. Cash flow is down, especially ours. And now this kidnapping business—it's likely to ruin us!"

"What? I like horses, but *my* welfare is more important than an animal's," Amelia groused.

Tony and Faith exchanged disapproving looks. He figured she wouldn't place money above an animal she loved any more than he would, but then again, neither of them had even a tiny fraction of the Langleys' wealth. And George was always complaining, no matter what his situation.

"Won't insurance pay the ransom?" Amelia was asking tersely.

"Only a small part," George returned. "True Heart was insured before we knew how valuable he was going to be, and we never got around to making the adjustment since the Derby."

"Maybe the police will find the damned horse, and we won't have to put up the rest."

"The police." George laughed, but he didn't sound in the least amused. "I hope they know what they're doing. They'd *better* be doing their job. It's up to them to investigate and ask questions, not Tony."

"George," Amelia said, her tone wheedling. "Did you ever consider Tony might be involved in this mess? I mean...considering his background. He left the New York scene awfully fast."

Tony stiffened at the reference, furious at the accusation. He waited for George to deny it, but the owner merely cleared his throat nervously. Damn it to hell! Tony figured he was the only person involved who cared more about T.H. than the money that could be won or lost on him. But that wouldn't matter to Amelia, who might have heard some gossip about him. Now that he thought about it, George's wife had been acting strangely distant of late. Noting Faith's frown, Tony wondered what she was thinking, when Harlan Crandall suddenly appeared in the hall behind them.

"Tony. Glad you're here," Harlan said, lifting a single brow when he noticed Faith. "Why don't we join George and Amelia."

The Langleys both looked uncomfortable as Harlan ushered the couple down the stairs. Tony was careful to keep his expression and tone devoid of his reaction to Amelia's offensive accusation as he made the introductions.

"This is Faith, a friend."

Tony wasn't sure why, but the statement felt right. Truthful. Avoiding Faith's last name was the same as lying, however. Tony was afraid they'd recognize it from the petition they'd all seen and discussed. They'd know who Faith Murray was soon enough, anyway, once they got a complete rundown from the cops.

"Faith, these are T.H.'s owners—Harlan Crandall, George Langley and his wife, Amelia."

"Sorry to meet under such trying circumstances," Faith said.

"Well, I'm sure you'll do your best to make Tony feel better, dear," Amelia purred with a false smile.

George didn't seem to notice his wife's animosity. "So what did you find out?" he asked Tony.

"Not much." After Amelia's crack about his being involved and George's reluctance to deny it, Tony wasn't about to share anything, not even his plans for leaving town. George could just figure things out for himself when Tony didn't show at the track the next day. "Did you find out where the ransom is supposed to be taken and when?"

"Thursday morning at nine at a truck stop on the outskirts of Beloit, Wisconsin," Harlan said.

Tony knew the small city on the Wisconsin-Illinois border was also on the way to Dubuque. Faith's expression told him she was aware of the fact, as well.

"When did you hear that?" George demanded.

"On my way here. The kidnappers called on my car phone, if you can believe it. These guys have all the information they need to keep us going." Harlan shook his head and for once lost his philosophical outlook. "Listen, Tony. About T.H.'s leg—does he have the hairline fracture or not?"

"I never got the chance to find out. It was still swollen when I checked on him late last night."

"Not good," Harlan said. "Depending on the way the kidnappers treat the horse, they could compound the injury, and then the animal will have to be destroyed."

Tony hated being reminded of the fact, one of the reasons he had such a sense of urgency about finding T.H.

"Of all the lousy luck," George muttered, "we'd be the ones to get saddled with it. I knew in my gut we'd never get another win out of that horse."

"You don't know any such thing," Faith said hotly. "And maybe you ought to be more concerned with the poor, defenseless horse and less with yourself!"

George, Amelia and Harlan merely stared openmouthed at Faith, who turned red to the roots of her hair. And Tony felt ashamed—first, that she had been the one to defend the colt *he* loved, and second, that he couldn't back her up. He couldn't lose his job—not now. He couldn't be left out of T.H.'s recovery, which was exactly what would happen if he were fired.

"I think we'd better get lost," he said. He took Faith's arm and squeezed it in warning. Then, to smooth things over, he asked his employers, "Anything I can do?"

"Local police and state patrols are on the job," Harlan said. "We might get a break any minute. Just keep in touch."

"Yeah, sure thing."

His favorite platitude, meant to appease when he had no intention of following through. Knowing he could only count on himself, as always, Tony steered Faith back to the car.

"So aren't you going to say it?" Faith asked as they sped through Barrington.

"Say what?"

"That I'm mouthy and should have kept it zipped."

"You only said what I was thinking myself."

Faith told herself to settle down. She was itching for a fight, though not with Tony this time. She was angry on his behalf. She hardly knew the man and yet had better insight into his nature than the people he worked for. He might be guilty of a lot of things, but how could anyone accuse him of stealing True Heart!

"You didn't tell me True Heart was hurt," she said, unable to keep the accusation from her tone.

He reacted with a steely, "No reason to."

"No reason? *No reason?* You tie me up, throw me into a stall, then take me hostage, and I'm not even supposed to know all the facts?"

"Now you know," he said tersely.

About True Heart, maybe. But about Tony? She had only a few clues.

Earlier, he'd avoided talking about the start of his career. Then Amelia's reference to his background made Faith think that what Tony hadn't said was far more important than the little bit he *had* said. Perhaps that was one of the reasons he was vulnerable and had developed such a hard shell to try to hide it.

But trying to figure out Tony would surely make her nuts. He must be schizoid or something—tying her up one minute, kissing her the next. Just remembering the embrace was enough to make her burn.

And not only in anger.

Faith told herself to get her mind off the man and back on the missing horse. "So do you think Harlan had a point?" she asked. "That the kidnappers might mistreat True Heart and ruin him for racing, even if they get their money?"

Tony's laugh was bitter. "That should make you happy since you wanna see him set free and retired." As Audra had stated in that letter.

"I just don't want him hurt." Though she was tempted to hurt Tony—she would have liked to punch some sense into him. "Whether through accidental injury at the track or mistreatment by a bunch of criminals," she went on. "Do you think a creep like Zak Hobson will take good care of True Heart?"

"If he wants the two mil, which I assume he does," Tony said. "At least Hobson's a groom. He knows what to do."

"Under normal circumstances," Faith added, distracted by the direction Tony was taking. They weren't going back the way they'd come. "Why didn't you tell George and Harlan about Hobson, anyway?"

"After Amelia's crack about my being involved? Looks like George isn't so sure I'm innocent, either."

Faith felt his hurt yet again and wondered about the past Amelia had referred to. But she wasn't about to ask. She didn't want to get any more involved with Tony D'Angelo than she already was.

When they whizzed by yet another road that would take them east toward the racetrack, she said, "You're going the wrong way."

"I know exactly where I'm going."

She didn't like the sound of that. "Mind filling me in?"

"Dubuque. I'm not waiting to find out about George and Harlan's cash flow or about a police investigation that's likely to go nowhere."

"You plan on going after the criminals yourself?" Faith's eyes widened when his jaw clenched. He was! "What if they're armed?"

Tony snorted. "Hey, I grew up in the Bronx. Gangs and drug dealers and the syndicate divided the borough into territories. Nearly everyone was armed. I survived that. I didn't lose my street smarts just because I left the old neighborhood."

Noting the Toll Road Ahead sign, Faith said, "Well, you can pull over and let me off at the side of the road. I've got enough street smarts to get myself home."

"I don't think you should be going anywhere by yourself—at least, not yet."

What? "Look, I gave you all the information I could." Irritation crept into her voice. "Or are you still suggesting I had something to do with True Heart's disappearance?"

He didn't answer directly. "You might tell the police or my bosses what I'm up to. I don't want anyone stopping me."

"I promise I won't tell."

"Yeah, right. Miss Mary Poppins lying to the authorities. I can see it now. Besides, think of this situation as protection. You never know what kind of dangerous characters you might run into trying to hitch a ride home."

"That's ridiculous." Not to mention incredibly high-handed of him! How dare he pretend to be thinking of her best interests—of ways to protect her—when he'd put her in this position in the first place? "These suburbanites are Milquetoasts," she said. "If I can handle someone like you, I can handle anyone."

He appeared somewhat amused as he glanced her way. "What makes you think you could handle me?"

His tone implied intimacies Faith didn't want to think about at the moment. Still, warmth spiraled through her as the powerful car swung onto the tollway. She glanced away from Tony's intriguing profile and forced herself to concentrate on the outrageousness of his actions. How dare he taunt her—not to mention keep her hostage—after she had tried her best to help him?

She remained silent. And plotted. She would get away from him if it was the last thing she ever did. Okay, so he was bigger and stronger than she. Not to mention that he was driving a car over seventy miles an hour. She wasn't dumb enough to try jumping from a moving car at any speed. As a matter of fact, she was smart enough to find a way to get him to stop the car. She'd wait a while, though. Let him think he'd won.

A few miles down the road, she groused, "Even a prisoner has to eat. I had breakfast before dawn, for Pete's sake, and it's almost sundown! My stomach sounds like a target range. If you don't feed me soon—"

"All right, all right. We'll stop at the oasis ahead and get some burgers. Don't get your panty hose tied in knots."

Faith suppressed a smile of triumph and pretended irritation she wasn't even feeling. "I'm not wearing panty hose under my jeans."

"No?" Tony flashed her a quick grin. "What are you wearing?"

"Wouldn't you like to know," Faith muttered, slouching down into her seat, where she continued plotting so she wouldn't think of more provocative images.

She tried not to worry that her heart wasn't exactly in her plan. The important thing was to get away from him, right? So why hadn't she even tried an escape attempt at Green Meadows? Faith rationalized, telling herself it was because she'd liked T.H.'s owners even less than his trainer and hadn't wanted to confide in them.

The Porsche quickly ate up the miles to the oasis. By the time they parked and headed for the building that spanned the tollway, Faith was keyed up and ready to make her move.

"So exactly how hungry are you?" Tony asked.

She figured she'd better be hungry enough to keep him busy for a while. "Two burgers, a large fries, a salad with garlic dressing, a chocolate shake and a box of cookies."

He raised his brows. "Sure you don't have room for something more substantial?"

"I think that'll be enough." And give her enough time, Faith thought, as she spotted what she was looking for. "Listen, I've got to, uh, use the facilities." She nodded to the door marked Ladies. "Why don't you go ahead and order, and I'll catch up with you."

"Yeah, sure thing," he said, the words and tone familiar. Hadn't he used them with Harlan and George?

Even as she entered the crowded rest room, Faith figured Tony was suspicious of her, as usual. That made her nervous. She'd figured she'd wait inside just long enough for him to be out of sight. And while he was standing in line for their food, she could sneak out and cross to the other side of the oasis where she could pick up a ride going toward the city.

Leaning back away from the door, she gazed out into the hall as another woman left. Coast looked clear. Faith took a deep breath and exited with a group of teenage girls. She grimaced when she spotted him—Tony stood opposite at the windowed wall. Nope. He hadn't gotten into line or ordered any food. He hadn't trusted her. So what else was new?

But his back was to her, Faith realized. If she were careful, she could make it.

Faith had barely walked three steps before stopping for a last look at the man who'd taken her hostage. His back was bowed and he rested a shoulder against the glass. He seemed so... dejected. He was staring out to the west, toward Dubuque, toward the heartland where she'd been born. And he was oblivious to the pedestrian traffic swirling around him. Able to see his profile, she was certain he was thinking about T.H. His rugged face was pulled into an expression that tugged at her heart.

He looked so forlorn. So lonely.

Once again, something about him reached out and touched her inside as he hadn't been able to do physically.

Faith told herself to go—this was her opportunity—yet she couldn't make her feet move.

Above all, Tony D'Angelo was alone. She suspected he'd been alone most of his life, had worked his way up on his own against greater odds than she had ever faced. But this was serious business. He was going after hardened criminals. Men who could hurt not only T.H., but him, as well. And he was plunging into territory unknown to him.

But not to her, a little voice said. She could help him if she wanted to.

But why should she? She shook off guilt that threatened to trap her. She had to think of herself. Had to get away. She even started to move. But then he turned and looked directly at her. Too late. She was caught by the hostile expression on his face that hadn't been there a moment before. The same expression he often presented to the world to protect himself.

Faith knew this because in his dark, fathomless eyes, she read a very different message—a silent plea she was certain he would never voice.

His movements deliberate, he stepped toward her, and she opened her mouth as if to object. Still mesmerized by his gaze, she felt no fear but couldn't make a sound. And then he had her, his strong hand wrapped around her upper arm, holding her fast. Her heart tripped in her chest and she told herself she'd missed her opportunity. Now she had no choice but to go to Dubuque with him in search of T.H. . . . raging rapids, sizzling fire, flying bullets or whatever.

Taking a deep breath, she tried to ignore the sensations his warm grasp was causing as she complained, ''Haven't you even ordered my food yet? Or are you trying to starve me to death?''

Chapter Four

"Relax, already." Unsmiling, Tony walked Faith toward the order line. "Women change their minds so much, I figured I'd wait and let you order for yourself."

She was certain he was lying, that he'd probably expected her to make a run for it and had intended to catch her. "Uh-huh, and we've already established what an expert you are on women."

He ignored the sarcasm. When they reached the counter, she told the fast-food server she wanted a burger, some fries and a shake.

"Lost some of your appetite?" Tony remarked casually, letting go of her to take some bills from his pants pocket.

She shrugged, trying to appear just as blasé. "As you expected, I changed my mind."

He ordered black coffee for himself and paid the bill.

"Aren't you hungry?" Unless he'd had a really huge breakfast early that morning, he hadn't eaten any more than she had throughout the day. "Straight coffee's pretty hard on an empty stomach. It could give you ulcers."

"I already have 'em."

Then he really should get something to eat, she thought, but didn't say so. The scowl on his face showed he probably didn't appreciate her concern.

He started to leave, hesitated, then turned back to the server. "Gimme a burger." He peeled off another bill. "For the road."

For the road.

Again, Faith realized she was actually going with him. With surprise, she also realized she was excited about the situation, insane though that seemed. She wasn't frightened of Tony anymore, hadn't been since she realized he was bluff and bluster outside and vulnerability underneath. She could handle him and was looking forward to going with him. They were going to save True Heart. At last she was going to take action that might make some difference to someone besides herself and her own little world.

For the road. Tony was escorting her toward the outer door when she suddenly remembered some responsibilities in her world that she had to take care of. She halted, making him stare.

"I have to call my neighbor and ask her to feed Lucy—my cat."

"Right now?"

"Why not? I don't know when or where we'll stop next."

He followed her to the bank of phones stretching along one wall and stood so close, he flustered her.

"What's the matter? Think I'm calling my cronies in crime?"

His breath feathered her hair and caused little chills to run up and down her spine. "I have to make sure you don't let anything slip. Don't tell your friend where we are or where we're going. Don't even tell her about the kidnapping."

For a moment, Faith thought he was being overly suspicious yet again. But then she remembered that he'd said he didn't want anyone knowing exactly where he was until he'd checked things out for himself. So she nodded as she punched in the number, wondering what excuse she could give Audra. She only hoped her neighbor was home. She breathed a sigh of relief when the receiver was picked up on the second ring.

"Hello, Audra?"

"Faith?"

Tony moved even closer. Faith tried to ignore the warmth emanating from his body, tried not to think about the kiss they'd shared earlier.

"Umm, Audra, I need to ask you a favor—can you take care of Lucy tonight? Make sure she has enough crunchies and fresh water and maybe give her a little canned food for a treat?"

"You're not coming home?"

Her neighbor sounded uneasy, so Faith attempted to perk up her own voice. "Well, I'm not coming back right away, but I'm okay." She paused. "If I don't show up by tomorrow, could you check Lucy again then?"

"Are you sure everything's all right?" Audra asked worriedly.

"I'm fine... really."

"Where are you?"

"Uh..."

"With a friend," Tony put in loudly.

Audra immediately reacted. "Who's that? A man?"

Tony took hold of the receiver and turned it toward his mouth. "I'm taking Faith out for a real good time. She's safe."

Appalled at the closeness he implied—Audra would be certain to demand every detail on her return—Faith refused to move away. She wanted to hear exactly what Audra would say.

"Wow, isn't this the horse guy?" asked Audra, sounding far more enthusiastic. "Tony somebody?"

"Yeah." Tony glanced at Faith questioningly. "How did you know?"

"She's always watching that Kentucky Derby tape. I've heard that gravelly voice of yours before." Audra laughed. "Of course, I never believed it was *only* your horse she was interested in."

Great—who knew what Tony would think now! Feeling her face flame in embarrassment, Faith struggled to get the receiver back, but he wouldn't let go.

"Faith said she was going out to the racetrack," Audra went on, laughter in her tone, "but I didn't know she'd really, umm, meet you so easily."

Tony's glance raked over her, and Faith knew what he was assuming. She knew what Audra was assuming, as well—that she'd picked him up. Not that her neighbor wasn't open-minded.

"Yeah, well, she walked right up and told me she had a big crush on me," said Tony. "I couldn't resist. She's pretty cute."

"Let go!" Faith gritted, her face burning as she finally ripped the phone out of his hands. "Audra..."

"Wow, you actually told him you had a crush on him? Right up front?" Audra had been telling Faith she needed some romance in her life for a long time. "Good work! You've got more guts than I thought."

"I didn't tell him I had any crush."

"Yes, she did," Tony added, leaning so close his nose touched Faith's.

Faith blushed harder and moved back an inch.

Audra laughed again. "Whatever. He got the right idea. Wow, congratulations!"

Faith knew Tony could still hear every word, and her face continued to flame. Furthermore, the way he gazed down at her, his eyes hooded, made it all the worse. She didn't want him getting any ideas... and she had to keep her mind on what was most important.

She cleared her throat. "One last thing, Audra. I may have to call in to work tomorrow and say I'm sick. Act like you don't know anything about it, okay?"

"No problem. You've been there for nearly eight years and never called in sick. They must owe you about a hundred and one sick days."

"Not quite so many, but enough. Just play it cool."

"Cool is my middle name. Have fun, Faith," Audra prompted with a sigh. "You deserve it."

After hanging up, Faith refused to even look at Tony as they walked out to his car. Uncomfortable, she expected him to give her a hard time about the crush thing and was amazed when he didn't say a word. And he actually opened the door for her like a polite gentleman.

Uncomfortable or not, Faith ripped into her burger and fries. She truly had been starving. Tony munched on his own burger and drank the coffee as he sped along the fast inner lane of the superhighway.

The sun set, splashing the western sky with shades of peach and rose. The horizon stretched on either side, for once not obliterated by tall buildings. Despite everything, Faith could almost imagine she'd launched herself on some type of adventure. Maybe it was the adrenaline zinging through her veins, but she felt freer than she had in years and years.

They'd gone several miles before Tony spoke. "So you've had a crush on me for a long time, huh?"

Her last bite nearly stuck in Faith's throat. "I don't have a crush on you," she said emphatically, knowing she sounded defensive. "That was purely Audra's imagination." She added, "I am not the type of immature woman who gets hung up on celebrities. I'm only attracted to men I actually know in person."

"So you think I'm a celebrity?"

What an egomaniac! "Well, you've been on television."

"Uh-huh. And you taped me," he commented, "then watched it every day."

"I taped True Heart. And I didn't watch that tape every day. Not that I didn't notice you or anything," she admitted. "I was impressed with what you said about True Heart. You sounded as if you cared about him. I even thought you were all-around personable and extremely enthusiastic. Of course, a television interview doesn't reveal the whole person."

"I'm even better up close."

She frowned, seeing a chance to burst his balloon. "No, you're much worse than I could have ever imagined."

He glowered, narrow-eyed, though she could detect he was also hiding some hurt.

But he deserved to feel hurt, she told herself. "If you think I'm sitting in this seat because I long to be with you, you're crazy. You're distrustful, defensive, high-handed and mean. You forced me to come along."

For a moment, he was silent. Then he snorted. "Forced you? Ha! You could have gotten away several times if you'd wanted to, Mary Poppins. You could have made a fuss at the Langleys'. You could have run out the door at the oasis before I turned around. But you didn't even try." His glance raked over her. "I watched you in the reflection from the window—you just stood there and stared."

So he *had* been watching her.

"I was trying to make up my mind."

"Deciding whether I was worth it or not?"

"Deciding whether this situation was worth it. I actually do care about your horse," she pointed out. "And I know the area you're heading for. I grew up there."

She might also add that she'd recognized Tony's loneliness and need, but she didn't want to hurt him that badly.

"You don't think I'm interesting in person at all, huh?" he asked, sounding a little disappointed.

She couldn't believe the way he kept bringing the conversation back to himself! "Will you please get over this personal thing?" Though his kisses had made *her* think personal. Remembering his hard chest, his warm lips, her pulse raced. "You took me hostage, tied me up in a stall. That wasn't nice!"

"Nice." He made a waving gesture and took the Porsche out around a truck, accelerating back into the fast lane. "Look, lady, you were in the wrong place at the wrong time. And I don't exactly trust too many people. I've had a rough life."

An apology? That was probably as close as he would ever get.

"Rough but rewarding," she commented.

"I lived on the backstretch for years," he continued. "You don't have any idea what that's like—it can be a helluva place. I started out as a hot-walker when I was sixteen. In the freezing winter, at Aqueduct in Queens. I worked my way up the hard way. I didn't even finish school . . . until a lot later."

Probably passed the GED, she thought, but she was more curious about what had happened to his family. "Didn't your parents object to all that?"

"My mother didn't know where I was. My father was dead."

So he *had* run away. "I'm sorry about your father." At least both her parents were living.

"I'm sorry about him, too. Have been for twenty years."

They drove on in silence, Faith thoughtful, if more at ease. At least she'd gotten Tony off the crush idea.

Some miles down the road, he pointed to a sign above the highway. "We'll be passing another exit in a minute or two. If you want, I can stop and send you back to the city in a taxi."

For a moment she was so stunned, she couldn't speak. "Now you want me to leave?"

"You've done enough to show your honest intentions, I guess. I can't find any reason not to believe you." He added, "If you could stay away from your place for a couple of days, though—sleep over at a friend's, keep away from work—I'd appreciate it. I wasn't joking when I said I don't want anyone to know where I am."

She considered her options, unable to keep from feeling disappointed. "I don't have any other place to stay. And I'm the type of person that the police would probably find if they looked for me. I'm not too good at sneaking around. Look how I managed to get myself caught on the backstretch."

He glanced at her closely, one brow raised. "So what are you saying? You *want* to come along?"

She didn't know why, but that's what her heart was telling her. "Maybe it would be best. And, as I already told you, I know Dubuque and the surrounding county."

Tony said nothing as he sped past the exit, eyes straight ahead. The sun sank lower and Faith yawned, her fatigue catching up with her after a long day. Tony's face was lit by the dim lights of the car's dash. He looked worried.

"I hope True Heart is okay. I really want to get him back," she said, that having been her main concern from the beginning. "It's probably silly of me, but I always wanted to do something that counted."

"Yeah?"

"Something heroic."

At least he didn't say that was stupid.

"I had silly daydreams as a kid," she went on. "You know, the ones where you ride up on some fiery steed and save the day?"

"Uh-huh, like the old Westerns where the hero rode off into the sunset at the end. Kind of lonely, though." Which was an odd statement for him to make.

"I didn't gallop off alone. I took the guy along, too. Love and justice triumphed. Everything was wonderful."

She expected him to laugh.

He didn't.

"So you still remember your old daydreams," he mused. "And I bet you can still dream big, can't you? You're lucky. Lots of people forget how."

Dream big? He sounded like he admired that. But she had to be honest. "I'm afraid I may be among that group who forgot how to dream. I haven't considered anything really wild and crazy since I was a kid. I've had to be too practical."

With her goals and her path all mapped out. She'd been following that practical road precisely . . . until today.

For some reason, Tony was bothered by Faith saying she couldn't dream anymore. He would swear she was the dreamy type—there was so much light in those beautiful eyes of hers, he could almost see them glow in the dark. She had obviously been loved and treated with respect. She was the type of person who *should* dream.

Now, he, on the other hand, was a different story. He hadn't been loved much and he hadn't been respected, but he'd dreamed, anyway—for many years his only escape from a miserable existence. And many of his dreams had come true. It was just that they weren't what he'd expected them to be. Somehow, they looked different up close, always had a darker side.

"It must have been some kind of a dream for you, winning the Kentucky Derby," she remarked, obviously having been thinking along similar lines.

"Yeah, sure was."

"It's not something everyone gets to experience."

"T.H. is one in a million," he said, giving credit to his horse the same way he did in interviews.

Her expression sober, Faith stared at the dark glass of the windshield. "I hope he's all right," she said again.

"Me, too." If T.H. *wasn't* okay, Tony was going to have the damned thieves' heads on a platter.

Faith yawned and leaned back against the headrest. Once again, he felt guilty for threatening her and dragging her around. He bet she was exhausted after all he'd put her through.

Though, he had to admit he still thought her presence a bit odd. He'd thought it unusual since he'd caught sight of her in front of his horse's stall that morning. Like all race-trackers, he was subject to superstition at times and had a strong belief in fate. Who was Faith and why did she pick this day to come visiting? Why did he feel this intense connection with her? A connection that went beyond sexual attraction.

He'd wanted her to come with him, had wanted her by his side, and his reasons couldn't be explained by all the excuses he'd already given her. He didn't even understand them himself.

He glanced at her again, watching her eyelids drift lower. If she fell asleep, he'd soon be driving in silent darkness.

"So you've got family in Dubuque County?" he asked, startling her awake with the question. "Is that where your parents' farm is?"

"Not anymore. They sold it and moved away."

"Hmm." She didn't sound happy about that. "What happened to your horse?" he asked.

"They sold him, too." She had loved that horse, if the emotion in her voice was any indication.

"You didn't object?"

"I couldn't object to selling Cochise. We didn't have any choice—my parents went bankrupt."

Bankrupt. That could do it . . . make her stop dreaming.

She sighed. "It happened a long time ago—thirteen years. I went to Chicago after I graduated from high school, got a job and started taking college classes at night."

"Weren't you eligible for loans?"

"I didn't want to borrow money, not after what my folks went through. Besides, I'm almost finished. I only have six more credit hours to go."

"And you also work full-time? Sounds like a long, hard haul." One which took guts and persistence, he had to admit. "Still, it musta made you restless. Maybe that's why you threw your rider this morning and jumped the rail."

"What?"

"I'm using track lingo. You're a runaway. You took off."

"I'm not running away. I'm only trying to help." She sounded uncomfortable.

So he wouldn't push it. But he could swear she was as caught up in that underlying, unspoken connection as was he. Where would it lead them? he wondered.

Faith didn't remember falling asleep, but when she awoke, the car had stopped and blue and white lights were blinking feebly above her. She gazed out the car window at a run-down motel and its buzzing, short-circuited sign.

A moment later, Tony strode from the motel office, got inside and started the car. "Only one room left. I guess there's some kinda convention in town—busloads of senior citizens who want to gamble on those riverboats."

Faith hadn't been to the Dubuque area since the gambling riverboats had been installed on the Mississippi, but the beginning of September had always been a good time for last-minute vacations.

Tony took the Porsche to the back of the motel, stopping in front of a door with flaking paint. She had no luggage— and would have to think about the problem of obtaining clean underwear and a toothbrush tomorrow—but in the meantime, she could think of nothing but stretching out on a bed.

A bed. Faith stared when Tony unlocked the door. "There's only one bed."

"There was only one room left," he replied. "I already told you that."

"I'm not sleeping with you." The words came out before she even thought.

"Then don't use the bed—that's where I'll be."

Faith glanced about at the other tired furnishings—a chipped dresser, a chair with a rip in its seat, a threadbare, dirty-looking carpet. There didn't seem to be any other comfortable places to lie down.

She cleared her throat. "Look, there'd better not be any hanky-panky—"

"I just want to sleep."

Not that she was a prude, she told herself, but she'd only known Tony for one day and still wasn't even sure she liked him.

She wandered into the bathroom, gazing at the sink, where an eternally dripping faucet had chewed a rusty stain in the enamel. "Weren't there any Holiday Inns open?"

"Excuse me," he said huffily. "I didn't know you demanded first class."

"Well, a cheaper motel would have been fine, too. I'm not that picky. I simply like clean."

"Look, I'm too tired to argue with you about motels, okay?" Tony locked the door and took off his jacket to sling it on the ripped chair. "Besides, I wanted to use cash—somebody could trace my credit card."

So that's why he'd rented a dump. Faith told herself she was also too tired to care where she slept—for this night, anyway. She sat down on the bed to take off her tennis shoes. Tony plunked down on the other side.

"I'm keeping my clothes on," she informed him.

"I'm taking mine off."

She gave him an outraged look.

"All right," he conceded with a sigh, "guess I'll leave on the pants."

Even so, she stared at his exposed chest as he removed his shirt—dark hairs swirled across it and downward, as if pointing to what lay below his waistband. As she'd expected, he was lean and hard and muscular.

He noticed her inspection. "Sure you want me to keep my pants on, Mary Poppins?"

Faith blushed. "I'm absolutely certain."

He yawned and pulled back the blanket and sheet, climbing into the bed, making himself comfortable.

"You're taking up all the space!" she complained, trying to figure out how she was going to lie down without touching him. "At least turn on your other side." So his back would be to her.

He complied, grumbling something unintelligible. Soon his breathing became heavy and even—he was asleep. Faith wandered about for a few minutes, tried to brush her teeth with a finger and some water in the bathroom, then washed her face.

When she came back to the bed, she turned out the bedside lamp and lay down gingerly. Though such carefulness did a fat lot of good. The ancient mattress sloped inward and slid her directly into Tony's warm back.

"Damn," she whispered, wishing she weren't so aware of the man lying next to her.

At least her fatigue would help her forget about him. Her eyelids felt like lead. Warmed by Tony's body, Faith started to drift off. She was nearly asleep when he turned, sliding his arm across her.

Her eyes popped open.

But maybe he liked to cuddle; she could tell he was still asleep from the sound of his breathing. She tried to relax again, tried to ignore the length of firm thigh lying against her own leg, the strong arm cuddling her, the breath warming her neck. She closed her eyes, imagined herself in her own bed at home, imagined Lucy curling up against her hip....

Her hip? Faith suddenly realized Tony had moved his hand downward, placing it on the rise of her hip. He murmured something, sliding his other arm beneath her and around her waist to press her body back tightly against him.

Her heart sped up and little thrills spun around in her stomach. And she was suddenly terribly uncomfortable.

They were way too close.

"Tony," she said softly, hoping he'd turn over again.

He didn't answer, at least not in recognizable words. He murmured again, patted her hip and slid his hand up and down her thigh. The thrills became heat. When his other hand moved from her waist to her lower belly, Faith caught her breath . . . and extricated herself, sitting straight up.

"Tony!"

"Wha . . ."

"Wake up!" If he wasn't awake already and trying to feel her up on purpose!

"What's the matter?" His voice sounded even thicker and more gravelly with sleep.

She turned on the bedside lamp. "You weren't keeping your hands to yourself, that's what's the matter! And if you can't behave yourself, you can sleep on the floor."

Tony blinked and pulled the covers over his head. "I'm not sleeping on the floor—I paid for this place. If you're so prissy, sleep down there yourself."

Great. What a gentleman! Faith stared at the icky carpet but rose to take a pillow and one of the blankets. She supposed it couldn't be any worse than sleeping on the ground. Throwing the pillow down, she wrapped the blanket around her like a sleeping bag and didn't even bother to turn off the light.

Let Tony do it—he paid for the place!

Chapter Five

Daylight came too soon. Squinching her eyes against the light, Faith pulled the covers over her face and tried to sink back into her dream of cuddling against a warm, hard chest.

Enclosed by strong arms, she felt protected . . . and desirable.

When her companion's mouth settled over hers, her own desire sparked and she kissed him back, sliding her hands along his heated skin. Their tongues touched, their breaths melded. He slipped a hand beneath her sweatshirt and up the length of her back to undo the clasp of her bra. More excited, she instinctively arched . . . while at same time she slowly realized she *wasn't* dreaming. . . .

She opened her eyes and gazed into the intent face of Tony D'Angelo. Eyes half-closed, he continued kissing her deeply, their limbs intertwined.

Tony D'Angelo!

What was she doing? Breaking the embrace, shoving at him hard, Faith sat up straight in bed. "What do you think you're doing?"

He groaned.

Faith glanced around wildly, refastening her bra. "How did I get here? You dragged me back to bed, didn't you?"

Tony yawned and ran his fingers through his mussed dark hair. "And good morning to you, too." He looked sleepy and even more attractive than usual, which infuriated Faith all the more. A little beard stubble only made the man appear rakish.

"How dare you drag me into bed with you!"

He frowned. "Geez, do you have to yell so early?" He looked around, as if he were assessing the situation. "And, hey, if you found yourself back in bed, you got up and climbed in all by yourself, Mary Poppins." He smiled. "Guess you wanted to wait until I was asleep to jump me. You should have just admitted you had a crush on me in the first place."

Faith shot out of bed like a rocket. "I didn't crawl into bed with you. I couldn't have!"

Tony raised a dark brow. "Sounds like someone isn't in touch with her libido, or whatever they call it."

Rather than listen to any more, Faith grabbed her purse, fled for the bathroom and slammed the door. Gazing into the mirror, she saw that sleep certainly hadn't made her any more attractive. There were dark circles under her eyes and her hair looked like a haystack that had been hit by a tornado.

Not that she should care. Still, she got her brush out of her purse, tackled her hair, then washed her face and tried to clean her teeth.

When she came out again, she glanced surreptitiously at Tony. Now dressed, he stood before the mirror above the

chipped bureau and shaved with a battery-powered razor.
He'd been more prepared than she for the fast trip. Resent-
ful of that, as well as his accusations about her libido, she
plopped down on the chair and shoved on her tennis shoes.

"Where are we, anyhow?" she asked tightly. "Illinois or
Iowa?"

"Does it matter?" But then he told her, "Iowa. Crossed
the Mississippi last night. This motel is on the outskirts of
Dubuque."

"Then I know where a Bulls-Eye is—a big discount store.
I need to stop and buy a toothbrush." Along with a few
other incidentals. And she'd better not have to beg him to
stop, either.

He finished shaving and placed the razor in a small black
bag he must have brought in from the car.

"My teeth feel like they're covered with green slime," she
complained.

"Yeah? They didn't taste bad. You don't even have
morning mouth."

She glared. "Look, I don't know what really happened
last night, but I don't believe you for a minute. I would
never jump a man."

He merely shrugged and opened the door for her. Chin
held high, she strode past, keeping plenty of space between
them. Once they were seated in the car, Tony peeled out of
the lot and headed off down the road. Glancing at her
watch, Faith realized the Bulls-Eye wasn't open yet, so she
suggested they stop to have a quick breakfast.

Tony chose another fast-food place, agreeing there was no
time to lose. While Faith called in to work—claiming she
had a terrible case of stomach flu and wasn't certain how
long she would be out—he munched on an egg sandwich
and rummaged around for a phone book.

"Damn," he muttered, "I shoulda taken time to look at the phone book in the motel."

Having finished giving her excuses to her supervisor, she hung up. "If you're going to search for the name Hobson, I know a better place to do so. The library will have a phone book for every town in the county."

"Good idea." Tony smiled crookedly. "I knew there was a reason I brought you along."

Still angry, she turned her face away.

He gave an exaggerated sigh. "Aw, come on, nothing happened in the motel. Don't be so uptight."

"I suppose I should be thankful you stopped me before I got too carried away," she said sarcastically, heading for the door.

The morning was full and shining. Even this far from the city, the air smelled clean and much fresher. And Dubuque was a pretty town, built on hills and bluffs above the Mississippi. Faith had always liked the area, but she couldn't exactly savor the surroundings this morning.

Tony opened the passenger door for her, then climbed in the other side of the Porsche. "Okay, I can see you're not going to relax." He turned to her before starting up the car. "You're right, okay? You didn't crawl into bed and jump me."

"I knew it! You dragged me in, didn't you?"

"Wrong again. I woke up and sat in the chair for awhile in the middle of the night. It's a habit of mine. Then you got up, staggered to the bathroom and crawled back into the bed."

She didn't remember any of it, but she felt a bit better. "Then you came back to bed."

"Yeah, but I wasn't trying to pull anything. I wanted to go back to sleep is all. If I really wanted to fool around, I would have started with you then," he pointed out.

Faith flushed, remembering the passionate way she'd reacted to him this morning when half-asleep. She wouldn't have thought she could lose herself so easily.

"I don't know why you're so uptight, anyhow," Tony groused, though he kept his eyes on the road as they drove along. "I'm not some kind of filthy ape. I'm even a gentleman—I stop when a lady says no."

"I didn't say you were an ape or anything." She thought him very attractive, always had, but she had no desire to give him the satisfaction of knowing so. "I simply don't like being accused of jumping you."

Or letting him think she was like all the other women he'd no doubt pursued. At least he hadn't called her "babe" after the lesson she'd taught him at the track. She sank back into the cushy seat, feeling vindicated.

"You know this town, right? I'll stop at the Bulls-Eye, then you can direct me to the library."

"Fine."

He said nothing more about that morning's incident until they found the discount store and pulled into its lot.

"I don't know why you're so freaked out about our being attracted to each other, anyway." Opening the door, he paused. "It's kinda natural."

"You're attracted to me? I didn't think I was your type."

His eyes slid over her casually. "You're not the usual, but you really are a cutie. And, hey, we both have hormones, right?"

She wasn't the usual?

Thinking about that one, she tightened her jaw and gave him a sharp look before opening her own door. "And we're both adults, as well. We're capable of keeping those hormones in check."

She intended to keep her hormones in check, anyway. She might be on a wild adventure, but she wasn't into wild affairs. She wasn't the type, and Tony wasn't *her* type. Both of them would need to be far more serious about each other for her to even consider the possibility.

Faith Murray was one smart young woman, Tony discovered as the morning went on. Not only had she thought of the library and its telephone books, she also had the librarian pull out detailed county maps. They made a list of every Hobson within miles—the name showed up in three towns—and did some photocopying.

Fresh from their morning clinch, Tony couldn't help being very aware of Faith as they worked closely together. He watched the light from the library windows gild her light brown hair with gold, and he took a big whiff of her flowerlike scent. She might have slept in her clothing, but she still smelled as fresh as a country meadow.

After a while, though, he began to get annoyed with the situation. Faith Murray was definitely pretty, but she shouldn't be on his mind every minute. If he didn't watch out, he was going to find himself hung up on her, something he wanted to avoid at all costs. For one thing, he still hadn't figured out her angle—she might not be a criminal or an animal activist, but he couldn't quite believe she had no personal reasons for agreeing to help him. For another, thirty-five and divorced, he was too damned old and cynical to be falling head over heels, a temporary euphoric state that always led to disappointment and heartache.

Tony scooted his chair over a few inches, putting more space between himself and Faith as she made the final list of Hobsons.

"I think we should check Green Oak first, then Webber," she suggested, not seeming to notice what he'd done. "Since Webber is thirty miles away."

"What about Dubuque? We're already here."

She agreed that Tony could try phoning but, as expected, Monday being a workday, no one was home. With a population of one hundred thousand, the place was too big to check out as easily as smaller towns, so they might as well head out into the country first. If they found no track of Zak Hobson in Green Oak or Webber, Tony reasoned, they could return and find the Dubuque Hobsons at home that evening.

They were walking toward the door of the building when Faith came up with yet another idea. "You know, Audra works in a department that has access to license-plate information."

"Meaning she might be able to trace the one on the trailer?" But Tony was reluctant. "If you call her, she might guess what we're doing. T.H.'s kidnapping will probably be in the morning papers."

"But it might not be a front-section story. Besides, Audra would want to help, and I know she can keep a secret. Especially if it involves the fate of an animal."

"You really think she could trace a license plate?"

"If she can't, she knows people who can help her. Her boyfriend is a computer hacker."

Still, Tony considered the possibility for another moment or two before giving in. "All right."

Since the receptionist might have recognized Faith's voice, it was Tony who made the initial call.

"Ask for Audra Neibauer personally. Say you spoke to her yesterday."

"Gotcha." Tony related that information and easily passed the receptionist.

Then Faith took the receiver from him, and Tony leaned close to listen. Once again, he became very aware of her, the curve of her cheek, the soft pink of her lips, the smooth, perfect skin that begged to be touched....

Eyelashes discreetly lowered, she seemed to be ignoring him, which annoyed Tony and made him feel bad somehow.

Audra's extension rang at least a dozen times. "Darn, I hope she hasn't put her line on phone mail."

But then someone finally picked up. "Audra Neibauer—how can I help you?"

And Tony became all ears.

"Audra, it's me again."

"Faith?"

"I know this is strange, but I have another favor to ask of you," Faith said hurriedly. "You told me your department could trace license plates, even out-of-state ones. Can you look for an Iowa license SVA and three numbers, one of which is a two?" She added, "If you won't get into trouble, that is. This is really important. We're trying to trace some stolen property."

"Uh-huh, and I know exactly what kind of property that is," Audra came back. "True Heart was kidnapped yesterday. I saw it on the front page of the morning papers."

Tony exchanged a startled glance with Faith. The front page? Geez, everyone in the city must know about the incident by now. And it would also be on the television news.

"I guess you're not just having a good time, huh?" Audra asked.

Faith took a deep breath. "The kidnappers are threatening to kill True Heart. We have to find him."

"Kill that beautiful horse?" Then Audra sounded determined. "Don't worry, that's not going to happen if I can help it. I'll get on it right away."

"I don't have to urge you to keep quiet about this, right?"

"Of course not. Get that horse back." Audra asked for the license numbers again so she could write them down. "I assume I'm looking for a truck?"

"Thank goodness you brought that up. A trailer, actually."

"I'll try both, just in case. Then call me tonight between six and eight . . . to be extra safe, at Sly's."

"The boyfriend?" Tony whispered.

Faith nodded, and Tony handed her his pen to write down the number. "Thanks. I really appreciate this," he told Audra, his mouth close to the receiver...and to Faith's lips.

"Tony?" said Audra, recognizing him. "You're welcome. And let me know if I can look up anything else on computer networks. Sly can break into almost anything but the Pentagon's files, and he'd love a challenge."

When Faith hung up, they headed for the door. Tony was worried. He stopped at a gas station, picking up a state highway map and a Chicago newspaper. He couldn't believe that the article stated the amount of T.H.'s ransom and hinted at the location where it was supposed to be left.

"Why would Harlan and the Langleys allow all this information to be printed on the front page?" he muttered. "Everything out in the open like that...not exactly the way kidnappers work."

"Those people didn't seem too concerned about True Heart."

"Harlan was concerned." At least he hoped so. "And he's smart."

But Tony didn't have any more time to muse about the owners' actions. Praying that they'd find T.H. fast, he drove for Green Oak, population eight hundred.

The land flattened as they got farther from the river, and the road was open and straight. Even knowing he could attract the highway patrol, he kept the Porsche at seventy. They were going to have to try to locate Hobsons in all three locations, if necessary, and all in one day. Every minute that passed could be the last for the greatest horse he'd ever had the pleasure of working with.

And he *was* going to locate T.H., if it was the last thing he ever did. Exactly what action he would take when that time came, though, wasn't clear. After all, it was just him and Mary Poppins.

He glanced at her, his gaze raking over the softly rounded figure, the bright eyes, the clear-cut features that could belong to an angel. His throat tightened, thinking about the danger they would surely face. Or rather, *he* was going to face. Tony already knew he was going to make sure Faith didn't get hurt. He felt extraprotective, probably because of all the head-over-heels stuff.

Damn! The woman made his hormones race no matter what he did . . . and in more ways than just physical.

"My family used to eat at a restaurant on the south side of the square," said Faith as they drove down the main drag of Green Oak, then around the park at its center. But that had been years ago and the building was deserted now. Other buildings were boarded up, some in such bad shape they seemed to be falling down. "There used to be a hardware store and a five-and-ten on the east side. But I guess everything is gone."

"Uh-huh," Tony agreed. "Place looks pretty dismal, like a ghost town. What happened?"

"Unfortunately, there are lots of small, rural towns in poor shape nowadays. They decayed slowly but surely over the years." She pointed to a concrete platform in the small park. "My mom said that bands used to play there on Saturday night in her day and that there was once a movie theater."

"Where was your parents' farm? Around here?"

"About ten miles away." She sighed. "They moved out of the county after the sale, and it's really too bad. Their parents grew up in this area, too. One of my grandmothers graduated from Green Oak High School. Not that that even exists anymore. All the kids in small towns were rounded up and bused to big, consolidated schools in the seventies."

"That kinda takes away from a town's spirit, doesn't it?"

Which was perceptive of him. "Sure does. But I guess people would be moving out of these agricultural areas, anyway. Farming has been in a slump for years. Young people usually go to college and get jobs in some city." They drove past a building with a big clock set under the eaves. "That used to be the town hall."

"Looks like the clock isn't working—unless it's nine in the evening."

"The building probably isn't used anymore, so nobody bothers to fix it."

"Hmm." Tony frowned behind his expensive-looking sunglasses. "Kind of disappointing. I thought these places were supposed to be all healthy and homespun, the kind of little burgs you see in movies with happy, healthy people and little kids and dogs running around."

"I'm afraid quaint little midwestern towns are fantasies for movies and advertisements," Faith explained. "In reality, a big percentage of the population of many small towns are the retired elderly. Then there are people from larger towns who buy houses in smaller ones because the taxes are cheaper. But they work someplace else and just sleep here, so they don't exactly add to the economy. Some people don't even know their next-door neighbors. That would never have been true when I was growing up."

"Too bad things have to change."

She glanced at him, thinking he was reacting in an unusually sensitive way. For *him*. "How come it bothers you?"

He shrugged. "Guess I always liked to think the heartland was special—a place where the small-town, all-American, independent spirit came from. You know, fried chicken, apple pie, the Fourth of July."

"Well, it was never quite so perfect—there are problems, and at least a few obnoxious people, everywhere. But at least farming and small towns were viable life-styles in the past. Sometimes it seems like the whole country is moving to the city. That's where the jobs are."

"If somebody wants to work with computers and corporate business and such," mused Tony. "I don't think I could. I don't know what I'd do if I didn't train horses."

"Interesting, but you are connected to the agricultural world in a way." She hadn't really thought about that.

"I'm real connected. Horses grow up on farms."

"I bet horse farms are fancier than the usual in this area, though."

"Mostly, but a horse also eats hay and oats and grass. Gotta grow that somewhere."

She realized they were heading out of town. The open fields were appearing again. She gazed longingly at tall corn rows and sighed. "I only hope this life doesn't become obsolete—like the plow horse when the tractor came along."

"Well, you're not exactly helping it survive yourself, are you?"

Startled, she frowned . . . because he was right in a way.

But instead of giving her a chance to respond, he slowed the car and did a U-turn in an intersecting gravel road. "We seem to have run out of town. I don't think we're gonna find any Hobsons sitting beside the road."

"Sorry. I should have been paying more attention." She'd gotten so involved in their conversation, she'd nearly forgotten their mission for a moment.

"It's my responsibility, too. Where should we start asking about Hobsons? The post office?"

"Not a bad idea."

Back in Green Oak, they parked the car in front of the small building with the U.S. flag waving out in front.

Faith took the lead, approaching the middle-aged man behind the counter. "Hi, are you the postmaster for Green Oak?"

"Dave Baxter, *acting* postmaster," the man told her. "They're going to shut these small places down one of these days. Already send all the mail to the nearest city and sort it by machine. People and jobs are expendable—"

"Is there anybody named Hobson in this area?" Tony cut in impatiently.

Baxter gazed closely at Tony, and Faith realized brash New York ways could easily annoy the postmaster. She gave Tony a warning look and tried to soften the situation. "We're looking for someone, Mr. Baxter, and we're not sure where they live." She smiled sweetly. "Are there any Hobsons in town or on the rural routes?"

Baxter seemed to relax a little. "Hobson? Well, once upon a time, I could've told you exact addresses—but there's that right-to-privacy thing now. All I'll say is there's a Mrs. Hobson on one of the rural routes."

"Does she have a husband or a son named Zak?" Tony asked.

"Don't know," Baxter said, shaking his head. "I don't live in Green Oak. I drive over here from Springton. Took the job when they cut back on help, laid people off there. I wouldn't have a job at all if I hadn't been working for the organization for twenty-two years," he said, anger in his voice. "Isn't that terrible? And all I have is a temporary job now."

Tony was beginning to appear visibly impatient. He told Faith, "If he doesn't know of any Zak Hobson, let's get going."

Faith took a firm hold of his arm. "We don't have to leave this minute, Tony," she said softly before turning back to the postmaster. "We appreciate your help. All this reorganization stuff is terrible, isn't it? But rural populations are getting smaller."

"And machines are getting too damned smart. Taking away people's wages—it isn't natural." Baxter smiled at her. "Do you live around here?"

Faith said no but mentioned her grandmother, which in turn launched them into a discussion of the stores that had once lined the square.

When Tony started drumming his fingers on the counter, Faith took hold of his hand. He raised his brows in surprise but settled down and didn't try to pull away. In fact, he seemed to enjoy the contact. Faith had to admit she enjoyed it—his fingers were callused and long, enclosing her own completely. In spite of herself, she felt a little shiver run up and down her spine.

Which she tried her best to ignore.

"This town really is deserted," she said. "No restaurant, not even a place to get a sandwich."

"You can get sandwiches and homemade pie at Shorty's Café over on the highway," Baxter told her.

"Shorty's Café?" repeated Faith, having noticed a combination gas station and convenience store near the edge of town.

"It doesn't look like a restaurant from the outside, but there's some booths in the store area."

Having gotten what she needed, Faith thanked the man again and led Tony outside.

"Let's head for that café. That's where the locals will be hanging out."

"It took you long enough to find out," Tony griped.

"You have to be nice to people in small towns. That man wanted to talk a little, and he might have known something important. You can't get all aggressive and impatient."

Tony didn't appear impressed. "Seems like a waste of time, but I guess I can be nice if you're gonna hold my hand during the process."

Not having realized she was still clasping his, she let go.

"Better watch those hormones," he teased, voice seductive.

She glanced away from his mesmerizing dark eyes. "Better watch your mouth."

Tony just laughed.

They headed for Shorty's Café and ordered coffee and pie. As expected, some local men came in, and Faith asked them about any Hobsons in the area.

A big gray-haired man in overalls nodded. "There was a Hobson west of town, yeah. Widow. She's in a nursing home in Dubuque now. Eighty-six or so, couldn't take care of herself out on the farm anymore."

"Does she have a son named Zak?" Tony probed.

The gray-haired man stared at him, probably thinking he was an outsider of some sort with his East Coast accent, designer sunglasses and razor-cut hair.

"Nope, Mrs. Hobson don't have a son. Two daughters."

"Did she have any relatives named Zak?" Tony continued.

"Not that I know of."

"A blind alley." Tony looked disgusted as he finished his coffee. "Let's hit the road."

This time Faith didn't object, though she still took time to say goodbye, give her thanks to the locals and compliment the café's hostess on the homemade pie.

In the car, back on the highway, Tony said, "Always polite, aren't you? Did you learn that in the country?"

"I learned it from my family."

"Though, I expect in a small town you have to think twice about what you do—if you want to get along."

"There are neighborhoods like that in every city, too, aren't there? Ethnic areas?"

"Yeah, some."

But he didn't seem interested in talking about it. Instead, he put his foot on the accelerator as they drove at seventy-plus toward Webber.

And Faith couldn't blame him. She only hoped a state patrol car wasn't sitting behind some highway sign. To keep her mind off that worry, she gazed at the passing fields.

"The corn is looking good. There must have been enough rain this year, and they'll get a decent crop." The window was open slightly, and she sniffed the incoming breeze. "And doesn't the country smell great? You should be out here in July on some warm night when the scent of alfalfa is in the air. It makes you feel like the night itself is alive."

"I'm getting the idea you really like it out here."

"Well, it's a nice place to visit," she admitted. "I usually see my parents at Thanksgiving or Christmas, plus one other time every year." Depending on her schedule and finances.

"But do you really like living in the city? Doesn't it make you feel kinda closed in—I mean, after all this space?"

How had he—a New Yorker—ascertained that? she wondered. "I wouldn't mind seeing a full sunset some days. Or a storm approaching. Fresh rain on the wind smells almost as good as ripe alfalfa."

"What kind of job are you preparing for, anyway?"

"Business administration."

"Which means you'll work for who?"

"Probably some big company."

"A corporation? That doesn't really sound like it would fit you."

"It'll fit," she insisted. She would *make* it work. "I want to earn a decent living with some security," she pointed out. "I work for a corporation now."

"Yeah, and I notice you're real broken-hearted about missing work."

Not wanting to admit she didn't miss a thing about it, Faith maintained, "This is an unusual situation."

"What do you want to do with the money from a better job?"

He sure was being inquisitive. "I can get a nicer apartment and have some free time. Maybe I'll take some vacations to some pretty places."

"What about a horse?"

"A horse? That would be very expensive. In addition to buying the animal... Well, you of all people know the upkeep expenses. And I'd have to buy a car so I could get out to where the horse was boarded."

"Look, if you're crazy enough about T.H. to come on a trip like this, you should definitely budget money for a horse. You're not gonna be happy otherwise."

His statement making her uncomfortable, Faith found herself getting defensive. "I can be happy if I decide to be. Besides, a horse might just be a symbol for me."

"Of what?"

"Freedom, elemental beauty—"

"I don't think you're gonna find that in a corporation."

"You can't say that for certain."

"I'm not saying some people can't find beauty in a big company—the ones who love machines and man-made schedules and the types who don't mind somebody breathing down their necks all day.''

Now she was distinctly ill at ease. "You don't know what I want. You haven't even known me that long."

"Maybe. But you can't tell me you'd be happy punching in and out on a time clock. Or settling for a bigger apartment and a little free time. Hey, if you're gonna dream, dream big. What about a whole house? What about that cowboy you were gonna ride off with? What about that horse?"

Faith simply sighed.

Sighting the sign for Webber, he slowed the car as they flashed past the Speed Limit Ahead sign.

Tony glanced at her, his face enigmatic behind the shades. "Well, dreams aren't what you think they are, anyway. Sometimes they're nothing but a bunch of hot air. Maybe you should be more practical from the beginning."

"Uh-huh."

Though Faith somehow didn't feel any better about that. Glancing out the window at houses with big lawns and huge trees, the quieter pace of rural life, she slumped a bit in her seat. After eight long years of struggling toward her goals, she didn't want to question them. And that was exactly what Tony seemed to be doing.

Chapter Six

Faith appeared so downcast, Tony immediately felt guilty, as if he'd stolen some little kid's candy or something. He thought he noticed her mouth tremble, and he saw the deep sadness in her big eyes. "But then, what do I know about other people's dreams and goals?" he said, trying to lighten the situation. "Not to mention what makes a person happy. I probably wouldn't be happy with anything or anybody, anywhere."

She gazed at him curiously. "I thought you liked your job—training Thoroughbreds?"

"I do...usually. It's not the horses, it's the other stuff that goes with the job that makes me crazy sometimes—people, pressure, animals who don't perform up to expecations. Or ones who get hurt." Which made him reflect on T.H.'s leg. "Besides, I'm in a bad mood over my stolen horse. You shouldn't take everything I say so seriously."

Not that he'd ever been the type of man who woke up with a big smile on his lips. But he wasn't ready to spill his guts to anyone, not even a Goody Two Shoes like Faith.

"You do what you think best about the future," he told her. "If you like corporations, fine. I just think that— well...a nice person like yourself should have something extra-nice in return. That's the only reason I was questioning you. Don't give up on the horse of your dreams."

Nice? Horse of your dreams? Geez, he couldn't believe he was saying such sappy stuff. But now she was rewarding him with a bright, sweet smile that warmed his insides.

"Maybe I *can* have a horse someday," she mused.

"Sure, and maybe other things, too. Like I said, dream a little bigger. You have to be practical, but you might be able to work out some kinda compromise."

Wouldn't hurt to give her a little pat on the back, he guessed. She'd do it for *him*. No matter how cynical he tried to be, no matter what he'd put her through, he had to admit she'd been more than decent.

She was way too decent a woman for him.

As if he should even be considering any type of romance....

To get his mind off the subject, he glanced around as they drove into the main part of Webber. This town seemed a little bigger than Green Oak but had the same sort of grouping of buildings surrounding a town square. Only a few of these buildings were being used—he spotted a craft store, a pharmacy, a video place, a bar and a grocery, among others. Some kids were playing on a swing set in the middle of the central grassy area and, beyond the whole scene, quiet, tree-lined streets branched off in all directions.

Faith spotted some activity on one of the side streets. "Look at all those cars and trucks. Something's going on. How about taking a turn over there?"

Tony complied, slowing to watch several men carrying paint cans and lumber into a run-down-looking house. Outside, two women washed windows, while a couple of others seemed to be offering lemonade and other refreshments to the workers.

"Think these people might know something?" he inquired.

"Doesn't hurt to ask. And we'll get the chance to field questions to a bunch of people all at once."

They parked and left the car. And since Faith could obviously handle the locals better than he, Tony let her take the lead in asking questions.

One of the women serving lemonade was talkative, informing them that the old house was being renovated by a community-service group and a couple of the town's churches.

"It's going to be a shelter." Slim and rather plain of face, she had a nice, friendly smile. "In this economy, some people find themselves homeless. Not to mention that there are always runaway teenagers and battered women who could use a roof over their heads."

"What a wonderful idea," said Faith.

Again, the woman smiled. "We think so. One of the radio stations out of Des Moines gave us a grant to get the ball rolling. Of course, it only pays for materials. The workers are donating their time."

As before, Faith patiently nursed the conversation along, letting the woman talk herself out. Thinking about runaways and battered women—small towns seemed to have their problems, too—Tony took the lemonade the woman offered and thanked her. More people filed in and out of the house, carrying various materials. The sound of hammering echoed from inside. On the porch sat a box labeled Donations.

"Does anyone named Hobson live in Webber?" Faith finally asked.

Tony immediately focused his attention on the conversation.

"Hobson?" The woman looked thoughtful. She turned, addressing one of the window washers. "Hey, Joan. Weren't there some Hobsons renting that house on Elm Street?"

"I believe so, some months ago. A woman and three kids."

"What about a husband?" Faith asked.

A man passing by said, "The Hobson woman's a divorcée."

Still focusing on the remark about months ago, Tony's heart sank. Even if the ex-husband were named Zak, the woman might not be found to hint at his whereabouts. He couldn't help putting his two bits in, though. "I take it these Hobsons no longer live on Elm Street, right? Where did they go?"

"I wouldn't know." From her perch on a stepladder, Joan waved in the direction of the town square. "You might ask at the tavern. Mrs. Hobson spent a lot of time there."

Tony wanted to head for the tavern right away, but he gave the conversation a chance to wind down. And Faith made certain that no one else knew more about the Hobsons—she even went inside the house to ask other workers. As she did so, Tony stayed out on the porch and stuck a bill in the slot of the donation box.

"Thank you," said Joan, beaming at him.

"No problem," Tony mumbled.

Faith came out of the door in time to notice, but she didn't say anything until they'd walked back across the lawn and slid into the Porsche. "That was nice of you."

"Nah, you're the nicey-nice person, not me." He met her questioning look. "I was a runaway myself—that's the only reason I put out the money."

"Which was a *nice* gesture," she insisted. "And I don't know why you don't want me to think so. Would you rather I continued to believe you were an arrogant creep?"

He covered his real feelings with a crooked smile. "I'd rather you thought I was a big lover-boy."

She shook her head. "Macho to the core."

But she didn't really sound serious or perturbed.

They stopped at the tavern, a dark place with no windows and an atmosphere that reeked of smoke and stale beer. Faith asked about Mrs. Hobson, but the bartender said he hadn't seen her for quite some time and didn't know where she'd gone. He also said that he wasn't sure what her husband's name had been but that Mrs. Hobson had had a drinking buddy named Rosie Brown who might be able to give them more information.

Filled with hope, Tony found Rosie's address in the telephone book and sped off with Faith to find her. But no one answered the doorbell.

Tony was so disappointed, he slammed his hand on the steering wheel when they got back in the car. "Damn it all to hell!"

"This doesn't mean the woman won't be home later."

"And what are we supposed to do in the meantime? Sit here and rot?" He added, "We don't even know if we're on the trail of the right Hobsons. And we don't have time to wait."

That is, T.H. didn't have time, he thought, worrying about all that front-page news.

"We'll just have to have faith. You said you had a hunch we'd find him. And we will."

He could believe that, gazing into Faith Murray's heavenly blue eyes. But Tony had to glance away, suddenly seized by the desire to take her in his arms and hold her, to have her hold him and never let him go. The yearning was sharp and more than physical... which made him highly uncomfortable.

He let out a big sigh. "So now what?"

"We could find a place to stay. We're obviously going to be out here another night. We can call Audra after six, then the Hobsons in Dubuque later this evening. We can try to call Rosie Brown, too. And once we line up a motel, we can also leave a note with our number under her door."

All good suggestions. But he couldn't help feeling frustrated, anyway. They were in a big hurry and the world around them was moving far too slowly.

Tony tried to distract himself by concentrating on more mundane needs. It was long past noon and they hadn't eaten lunch. He drove to a restaurant he'd spotted when they'd entered the town. They went in and ordered hot meals.

Obviously hungry, though she hadn't been complaining, Faith munched on the salad that came with her chicken-fried steak. "Why did you run away from home?"

He frowned. "Why are you asking me that?" And why now?

"I'm curious. I've been thinking about it since you left that donation."

He still wasn't into spilling his guts, but he supposed it wouldn't hurt to be honest with someone who wasn't trying to pull anything. "I told you my father died when I was a teenager. My mother remarried and my stepfather and I didn't get along."

"He was mean to you?"

He gave a bitter laugh. "Mean? That's not a strong enough word. He beat the living hell outta me."

Faith looked appalled. "How awful! What about your mother? Didn't she know?"

"Yeah, she knew."

"And she didn't want to get away from such a horrible man? To stop him from hurting you?"

"I suppose she might have thought of it, but she was too dependent."

"Or afraid," said Faith. "Your stepfather might have been beating her, too."

Tony didn't like to think that was possible. "I never saw him lay a hand on her. If I had, I might have gone to reform school instead of the track." Which was more than his mother had tried to do for him, he supposed. "I headed for the track, where me and my pop had had a good time a lot of weekends. He always said that horses were trustworthy and had heart. They gave you their all, were better than people."

The waitress arrived with the main courses. Digging in, Tony was happy to push old memories aside.

"Have you tried to get in touch with your mother since you left home?"

He'd relaxed too soon. The memories were back. "I contacted her once, several years later. She was still married to the jerk, though."

"She must have been very afraid. People get caught up in situations like that."

The way she was looking at him made Tony uncomfortable. He didn't want anyone's pity. "I don't need it psychoanalyzed," he grumbled, hoping she'd give it a rest. He'd dealt with the hurt and loneliness in his own way.

She gazed at him oddly. "Do you have any brothers and sisters?"

"No."

"Aunts? Uncles?"

"Probably somewhere, but I never kept up with the family thing." He guessed he'd have to be more direct. "Now, can we stop this line of questioning?"

She raised her brows. "Well, okay."

Figuring she'd get back to his past if he didn't change the topic, he said, "About that shelter—do people out in the country always try to take care of their own like that?"

"I think there's more of a sense of a community here than in the city, even with dwindling populations and neighbors you don't know. When someone passes away, friends and acquaintances usually bring food to the house of the bereaved family. And when there's a fire, people often take up a collection."

"So they show some responsibility."

"Because they're more likely to know each other. It's easy to think of yourself as anonymous when you're surrounded by millions."

Tony certainly didn't feel anonymous with Faith. In fact, he realized, he felt different than he'd ever felt with anyone before, as if they were communicating at some deep level. Probably because she had made a stab at trying to figure him out. Though why she would want to do that, he didn't know. But he didn't have time worry about it, he told himself, finishing up his meal.

They weren't on some date or something; they were on a mission.

If Faith had guessed where Tony was coming from before, she was even more certain of a troubled past now. The background that had shaped him had left him without a family or a community, unless one counted the backstretch workers at a racetrack. And they were a transient lot. With a childhood like his, it was no wonder he didn't trust anyone.

Before they left the restaurant, they asked the waitress about local motels. The woman said there were a couple, but suggested they try a farmhouse bed and breakfast instead. The place wasn't listed as such in the phone book yet, since the couple who ran it had just started the business.

No doubt thinking it would be perfect for their purposes, Tony asked Faith if it would be okay and then called to make the reservation. She had to smile at the change in their relationship—the day before, he hadn't even asked her if she wanted to go to Iowa. She also noted that he requested two separate rooms and was appalled that she had mixed feelings about that.

She didn't really want to have a romance with Tony D'Angelo, did she? Was he growing on her? If so, she'd better put a stop to her burgeoning feelings before they got away with her. He might not be as bad as she'd thought at first, but he wasn't the type of man she was looking for, even if his kisses made her toes curl and her knees go weak.

They drove back to Rosie Brown's house, but the woman still wasn't there. Faith wrote a note with the number of the bed and breakfast and stuck it under the woman's front door. Then, restless, Tony drove her around town and explored several of the roads outside of Webber. They stopped for gas, coffee and some other incidentals at a grocery store.

Tony was hyped for Faith to call Audra at six on the dot. He stood near the pay phone in the grocery-store lot but didn't hover over her and try to listen to every word as he had before...until he realized she was hearing startling news.

"What?" Faith blanched, her blood running cold. "The police came to Pilgrim Insurance looking for me?"

"Afraid so," Audra told her, seemingly less upset over the incident than she. "I think there might be a warrant out for your arrest. They questioned me." But she hurried on, "Don't worry, I kept a stone face. And I told them the truth about not seeing you since Saturday night. But I've got more important news. I traced that trailer license you're looking for—it belongs to a company called Crandex Corporation."

"Crandex?"

"Crandex!" repeated Tony, looming over the phone. "That's a business that's owned by Harlan Crandall and George Langley."

"Oh, my God!" murmured Faith.

The horse theft was an inside job!

She could tell Tony was thinking the very same thing. And he looked nearly as apoplectic as he had when he'd first seen T.H.'s empty stall. Distracted and upset, wanting to do something to comfort the trainer, she hardly listened as Audra went on.

"Faith, are you listening to me?"

She forced herself to tune in as she watched Tony pace up and down. "I'm sorry. What did you say?"

"Is there anything else I can do? I want to help you." Audra was sounding pretty emotional herself. "You're one of the kindest, sweetest human beings I know. Somebody's trying to get you into trouble, aren't they?"

"Maybe some people saw me at the racetrack with Tony. The police questioned me because I sneaked onto the back-stretch." But she wasn't about to tell Audra about the rough way Tony had treated her in the beginning. "Please don't worry. We'll get things straightened out."

"You found the horse?"

"We have a lead, and the information about the trailer helps even more."

At least, Faith hoped so. She ended the conversation by assuring Audra that she and Sly didn't need to rent a car and

drive to Iowa to rescue her. Audra, in turn, said that Faith's
cat was fine and that, if she wanted to, Faith could call Sly's
apartment again at six the following day.

As soon as Faith hung up, Tony impatiently grabbed the
phone.

"What now?" she asked, but he was already busy
punching in numbers.

He gestured for her to wait for a moment. Actually, several moments—although he said nothing, Tony listened intently. When he finally finished, he shot the receiver back on
its hook and just stood there.

The stunned posture scared Faith even more. "Will you
please talk to me? What's going on?"

Finally he seemed to become aware of her presence. "I
have to take you back to the town square. Then you can find
the police. Or the sheriff. Whatever. Tell them I kidnapped
you and took off."

He was going to leave her behind? Her response was a
vehement "No way!"

"Look, the adventure is over. This is serious. I called my
answering machine and got an earful. First, messages from
Harlan and George asking where the hell I am. Then a
warning from my assistant trainer—the owners told the police they think I've got T.H."

"But you don't!" Having come to know Tony as well as
she had, Faith was indignant for him. "They're framing
you!"

"And one or both obviously had their own animal stolen...though God knows why. Insurance? I didn't know
either of them was in financial trouble." Tony ran a nervous hand through his hair and focused on the horizon.
"The colt may already be dead, you know. There wouldn't
be much reason to keep him alive. No wonder they spilled
all the details to the newspapers."

"They can't get away with this!" She wanted to cry...and to put her arms around Tony, though she dared not encroach on his space, considering his foul expression.

"They've got a lot of money and clout, Faith. I've seen things like this happen before."

"But I'm a witness!"

"Uh-uh. You're an accessory. At least, that's what they're trying to prove. They had everybody at the track questioned. Several people saw you with me. I guess Mrs. Langley was especially suspicious of you." He placed a hand at her elbow and walked her toward the car. "That's why you've got to tell the cops I kidnapped you. Tell them you don't know why, but I was acting crazy. You were lucky you talked me into letting you go."

Her heart postively wrenched at the thought of leaving him alone in this. "I'm not going without you, Tony."

"You don't owe me this."

"Oh, yes, I do." She turned to face him when they reached the car. "And I owe it to me. When something's wrong, a person has the responsibility to try to set it right."

"You're too idealistic."

"It's not idealism, it's ethics." Not to mention her growing feelings for him. He unlocked the passenger door so she could get in. "I'm warning you, Tony, I'll tie myself to the seat with the seat belt before I let you abandon me on Webber's town square."

He rolled his eyes.

And she couldn't believe she was so passionate about a man she hadn't even known a few days ago.

"You don't know for sure that T.H. is dead," she insisted as he started the Porsche and pulled out of the grocery-store lot. "We can still find Zak Hobson, I'm sure of it. And we'll do what we have to do to get the horse back."

Tony made no response to that, though he didn't return to downtown Webber. Instead, he stopped at a bank drive-through to use a cash machine, then nosed the Porsche down the road in the direction of the bed and breakfast.

Faith let out a soft breath of relief.

"The highway patrol probably has a description of this car, as well as of you and me."

"Then we'd better keep to the back roads—county blacktops and gravel." Again, she tried to be encouraging. "Don't let them get away with this, Tony. And don't worry about me—I want to help."

He sighed. "Okay. But be prepared if and when the cops do catch up with us. I'm gonna tell them I forced you to come along, and you'd better agree."

Faith wasn't sure what she'd do in such a situation and she tried to put it out of her mind as they sped down the highway, then turned off onto a gravel side road. They arrived at the bed and breakfast about twenty minutes later. A beautiful white farmhouse with porches on all four sides, the building sat on a hillside dotted with huge maples and elms and offered a commanding view of the countryside. Herefords grazed in the pasture across the road and, though it was now twilight, the animals' red coats glowed against the green of the grass and trees.

But neither Tony nor Faith was in a good enough mood to enjoy such a setting. He was careful to park the car out of sight behind some bushes before they walked to the door.

The pleasant-looking middle-aged couple who ran the facility greeted them.

"How do you do? I'm Velda Ellis," said the woman. "And this is my husband, Bob."

"Hi." Tony offered his hand. "I'm Jack Smith, and this is my fiancée, Hope."

Fiancée? Faith tried not to show her surprise. She also wished Tony had given her some warning about what he was going to say, and that they'd be using fake names.

But Velda Ellis was very enthusiastic and friendly. "You're only our second set of guests, so you'll have to forgive us if we forget anything." She immediately stiffened. "Oh, dear, speaking of forgetting things, I didn't put any towels in your quarters."

"Don't worry about it," Tony assured her. "We're casual."

Very casual, considering they had no luggage, Faith realized. She hoped that didn't look too strange. She also hoped she didn't look too rumpled in her sweatshirt and jeans.

Bob took his leave before Velda gathered some towels and showed them to their rooms, a separate suite on the opposite side of the house with two bedrooms connected by a central sitting room.

"That leads out onto the porch," said Velda, pointing to the glass-paneled door in the sitting room. "There's a big old swing out there if you enjoy such things." She glanced at Faith. "You're on vacation?"

Faith nodded quickly. "Right."

"Then you'll want to know all about the sights around here."

Which the woman would probably be more than willing to tell them about right at that moment. To discourage her, Faith forced herself to yawn, feeling guilty as she did so.

"But if you're too tired, we can talk in the morning," said Velda, getting the hint. "I've also got a bunch of brochures I can give you at breakfast. Is there anything you don't like in the food department?"

"Anything's fine with me," Faith said.

Tony added, "We're not picky." He spotted a telephone on a table near the wall. "Can I use that phone? I have a phone card."

"Certainly. Local calls are on the house, of course."

"And I can pay you for the rooms now, if you want," he told the woman. "Since we're only staying one night."

"No problem. After breakfast will be fine."

Velda left, and Tony raised his brows, looking at Faith. "Trusting, hmm? How does she know we won't sneak out before dawn? Or that we'll really use a phone card or that we won't call Australia? They should get a deposit first and they shouldn't put phones in the guest rooms at all."

But he didn't wait for a reply as he took the receiver off the hook and placed his phone card on the table while he punched in the numbers. Faith sat down on a comfortable chair and laid her head back, trying to relax. She listened as Tony reached the Hobson residence in Dubuque, gathering that the person he talked to wasn't Zak and didn't have relatives by that name.

"Damn." Tony replaced the receiver as he glanced at Faith. "I don't think the guy was lying, though. I think I woulda been able to tell."

Next he tried Rosie Brown's number, but the woman still wasn't home.

"You're really tense," Faith told him, his hyper mode getting on her already frazzled nerves. "Why don't you sit down for a while?"

"Sit? I don't even think I'll be able to sleep tonight."

"Too bad. The bedrooms are lovely—four-posters and high ceilings." She'd glanced in as they'd entered the suite.

Tony paced back and forth, then went out the door onto the porch. Feeling for him, Faith rose and followed, taking a deep breath of fragrant, fresh air. Tony leaned against a porch column. Night had come on, and above them, the sky was thickly studded with stars.

"How beautiful. You can't see stars so clearly in the city." Which Faith had always missed terribly. "It looks like a cloak of diamonds thrown over the earth."

"Or sequins. Maybe the universe is cheaper than you think."

"What a cynical thing to say!" she said, poking him. "This is no time for your negativity, Tony. You should try to be positive."

"Sure. My horse is missing, probably dead. My career is ruined. Maybe I'll even go to jail."

"I don't believe T.H. is dead," she said stubbornly. "And you are not going to jail, not if I have anything to say about it!"

"He's not even my horse," Tony went on, "though he ran for me. He has a heart like a lion."

"We'll find him."

"If the cops don't find us first. Or the FBI. God only knows who the Langleys and Harlan called in on this."

"Can't we try to explain things if the authorities do catch up with us?"

"Why should they believe us? We took off."

"Because you were desperate to rescue T.H. I do think it's a bit strange that you feel you have to do everything on your own, though," Faith had to admit. Things might have been different if he'd shared his suspicions with the police. "Is there some reason you don't trust the authorities?"

"I told you, money and clout can get you everywhere. Two reasons I'm no longer training in New York."

"You didn't move into the Midwestern circuit because you wanted to?"

"The wife of one of the owners I used to train for in New York got me in hot water."

Uh-oh. Faith wasn't certain she wanted to hear more about his lover-boy escapades. "You came on to her?"

Tony snorted. "Hardly. I turned her down. But she managed to get even when her husband walked in on the little tryst she had planned. She told him I tried to force my attentions on her. In turn, he told me they didn't want to make a scene, of course, being high mucky-mucks in society. He just suggested I hit the road and never look back. He would make certain his friends got the word that I was not to be trusted. I had to start all over again—it was either the Midwest or California."

Faith digested the information. "I don't understand. Why didn't you stay and stick it out?"

In the semidarkness of the lighted windows behind them, he turned toward her. "You believe me?"

"Why shouldn't I?" She'd been nose to nose in bed with the man and he'd backed off easily enough. "And I also think you have so many choices in the girlfriend department, you would hardly need to force a situation. Anyone with any sense would know that."

Suddenly he was looking at her with great interest. "I thought you said I was obnoxious and all that stuff."

Faith became nervous enough to back away a tad. Breathing room, she told herself. "But you're good looking and . . . well, you have your own sort of charm."

He smiled and moved closer. "And you don't seem to think I'm dangerous."

"I was scared when you caught me in the barn and threatened me. But after a while, I started to realize—" She hesitated to say what she'd actually thought.

"You realized what?"

How did one address a man's vulnerability diplomatically? "You have a tough exterior, but I don't think you're that tough inside."

He stared off into the darkness, didn't say anything.

While Faith remembered Mrs. George Langley and the nasty things she'd said about Tony. "Do you suppose Mrs. Langley heard about your problems in New York? Was that the trouble she was referring to?"

"It was supposed to be kept hush-hush, but who knows what got spread around."

He continued standing, leaning against the porch column. Distress and sorrow seemed to radiate from him, making Faith yearn to take some of it away. He'd been betrayed more than once in his life. Without thinking, she reached out and stroked his arm.

"Are you trying to comfort me?"

"I'm showing I care."

"Oh, yeah? How much?" He grabbed the stroking hand and drew her closer.

"Enough" was all she would say, though her pulse sped up.

She didn't balk, however, when he pulled her against him, taking her in his arms. And she didn't object when he angled his head to kiss her, at first softly, then more deeply and passionately. Her pulse racing, she wrapped her arms about his neck, reveling in the sensation of his heart thudding against her chest. Murmuring soft words, he ran his fingers through her hair and kissed her cheeks, her forehead, her chin, before moving back to take her mouth.

Aeons seemed to pass. More aroused than she'd ever been in her life, Faith clung to Tony, her breathing rapid and shallow. When he slipped a hand beneath her sweatshirt, his fingers left trails of fire. She began to think that second bedroom was a real waste of money....

And then she nearly cried out when Tony stopped suddenly, lifting his head to gaze down at her.

"If we keep this up, I'm gonna make a move on you—try to get you into bed."

"You want to make love?" Their minds had been on the same track.

"That's a pretty way to put it."

And even mentioning the word *love* might threaten him, Faith suddenly realized, hastily attempting to calm her desires. Also, she'd be allowing herself to get involved with a man who openly admitted he didn't want a long-term relationship with a woman. She would be hurt. She would need some kind of promise, she knew, before getting physical. Reluctantly, she slid her arms from his neck.

As if he knew what she was thinking, he also moved back, putting space between them. "Good idea. Keep your distance, Faith. I'm no good for you. I've been through the mill, been through a messy divorce, pretty much plan to remain single for the rest of my life."

Remain single? What on earth was he talking about? "I didn't hear myself proposing to you," she said indignantly.

Which made him laugh. "You got a mouth on you, even if you do have that sweet, innocent heart."

"I told you a long time ago I'm not so innocent."

"Uh-huh, a real long time—yesterday." He crossed the porch and opened the door for her. "Now let's try to catch some Zs. I want to get up early tomorrow morning."

Faith headed for her bedroom, then turned to look back. Tony had also paused to stare at her, but when their eyes met, he raised his brows, then headed for his bedroom and closed the door.

She felt bereft.

Which was ridiculous. She was allowing herself to get far too attached to the man.

But the thought of leaving him made her feel even more awful. Otherwise, she would have taken him up on his offer to drop her at the Webber town square.

What had she gotten herself into? Was she crazy? Faith wondered, now aware that her heart was as much at risk as the job and reputation she might lose if the police caught up with them.

Once again she reiterated the main reason she'd come on the trip—she wanted to rescue True Heart. Added to that, she conceded, was her attraction to heroic outdoor adventure, especially after years of leading a quiet, busy city life. Although it was difficult, she had to think of Tony D'Angelo as a partner, not a lover, no matter how his kisses had thrilled her. As an avowed playboy, he couldn't be trusted.

Speaking of trust, Faith wondered if Tony could even be relied upon as a partner. What if he got up at dawn tomorrow and tried to sneak off without her?

The very thought was no incentive for sleep, dead tired though she was.

Chapter Seven

"You look a little wrung out," Tony told Faith the next morning when she showed up for breakfast.

Placing a plate of toasted muffins on the table, Velda Ellis immediately appeared concerned. "Oh, dear. Were the rooms too warm? I didn't think the air-conditioning was necessary this September, since the nights have been cool—"

"The rooms were wonderful," Faith cut in, glaring at Tony. "I was just restless."

And it was all his fault!

She hadn't gone so far as to peek into Tony's bedroom, but she'd been up and down several times during the night, once taking a hot shower. Perhaps it should have been a cold one, though, after Tony's steamy kiss. She was angry that he could create that sort of reaction in her, could make her fret about him all night.

And then he had the audacity to tell her she looked bad the next morning!

She glared at Tony. "You don't look so hot yourself."

Velda widened her eyes. Poor woman.

"We always bicker," Faith explained, trying to cover. "Don't we, *Jack?*"

Tony didn't blink an eye. "Yeah, we sure do, *Hope,* but I guess that's what makes our relationship interesting."

Who knew what Velda thought of all of this, but the woman went back to the kitchen to fetch more coffee. Her husband having left earlier that morning, Velda was playing hostess on her own. She had served a tasty omelet breakfast while chattering on about the county's history. Faith listened politely, though she already knew about most of the historic old houses, as well as Dubuque's riverboat museum and the statue that honored the county's French founder.

Tony also behaved politely and didn't act openly impatient about eating fast and leaving, though Faith couldn't tell if he was truly calm or merely subdued. He'd even made some small talk.

"How did you get into the bed-and-breakfast business, anyway?" he asked Velda when she returned with the fresh pot of coffee.

The woman sat down on the other side of the table. "Oh, I like meeting new people and, since our last daughter graduated from college, this house was feeling a bit big for Bob and me. We love living in the country," she went on, "and we love this house—it belonged to my parents and their parents before them. But sometimes it feels isolated out here. Having guests from time to time is perfect. We had to do some renovating, but it'll pay for itself."

"You've got a real nice place," said Tony.

"Why, thanks."

"Though you might want to fix the lock on that door that goes out onto the porch in our suite. I noticed it was broken last night."

"I appreciate your telling me about it." Velda laughed. "But we rarely lock any of the doors, so it doesn't really matter."

Tony appeared startled. "You don't lock the doors?"

"I know we should, that the country isn't safe like it used to be years and years ago, but I simply can't bring myself to change. I grew up trusting people, and I don't want to give that up."

To his credit, Tony didn't tell the woman she was out of her mind, though Faith thought he looked as if he wanted to.

The phone rang, and Velda rose to answer it. She'd only exchanged a few words with the caller when she turned to Faith. "It's a woman named Rosie Brown who wants to talk to you."

Faith gave Tony a warning look as he was about to bolt out of his chair and follow her. There was no need to make Velda suspicious and give her reason to mention them to the authorities.

Faith talked to Rosie, who gave her information that made her heart sing. She thanked the woman profusely and wrote everything down as she tried to remain calm. Then she walked back to the table, smiled at Tony and asked him if he was ready to leave.

"Sure am." He pushed his chair back and threw his napkin on the table. "Great breakfast, Velda. We enjoyed staying here."

And along with the price of one night's stay, he gave her a few extra dollars.

"You don't need to do that," the woman objected.

"Please, your service and this place are worth it," Tony told her with a big grin.

He must have been ready to burst, but he waited until they were safely in the car to hear Faith's information.

"Rosie said that Naomi Hobson lives in the trailer park in Springton, seven miles west of here. Naomi's divorced, but her ex-husand's name is Zak—"

"Yes!" Tony made a gesture of victory and peeled out of the driveway. Then he roared off down the gravel road, spraying rocks and dust on either side.

"Now we only have to pray that Naomi knows where Zak is."

"She will!" Tony insisted, looking intense. "My hunch is back. We're gonna find T.H. and rescue him if it's the last thing I ever do."

Wanting to believe Tony was right, Faith was happy to see him brimming with enthusiasm for once. Her own hope surged as well. And at least the news from Rosie had turned her thinking back toward the rescue of T.H. . . . and away from some ridiculous, romantic notions she was getting about Tony.

Traveling the back roads to Springton took a little longer than reaching it via a main highway, but Tony agreed that doing so was best. The place wasn't any bigger than Webber, but Faith suggested he stop at a service station to ask directions to the town's trailer park. Tony figured he could find it by himself, but he supposed asking could save some time.

As they entered the station's building, two locals in billed caps stood at the counter talking to the service attendant and drinking coffee. One of the dudes had lanky brown hair and a dirty T-shirt, while the other was beefy and didn't look much cleaner. They both stared, though Tony paid them no mind.

He addressed the service attendant. "Which way to the trailer park?"

"East," cut in the man with lanky hair.

"East." That helped a lot. "Which way is that?"

"Don't know your directions, huh?" The beefy man guffawed. "Must not be from around here."

The service attendant chortled. "That ain't hard to tell, Paul. Not with that accent."

None of them were being helpful, which made Tony not only impatient but angry. "I guess you guys *are* from around here," he said, not bothering to hide his sarcasm. "But that don't mean you know which way is east."

The beefy man straightened and narrowed his eyes. "Hey, you calling us stupid?"

"I didn't say the word *stupid,* did I?" Tony wasn't in the mood to back down.

Face flushed, Mr. Beefy stepped closer. "Well, you're acting pretty smart-mouthed, joker—"

Then, before Tony could react, Faith suddenly slid between them. "Please." She smiled sweetly at all three locals and placed a hand against Tony's chest. "We're late and we need to meet someone." Then she grabbed Tony's hand and squeezed it. "Aren't we, honey?"

As before, when she'd taken his hand in the Green Oak post office, Tony was momentarily disconcerted. Faith could probably get him to agree to anything. He managed to nod.

And Faith made a waving gesture. "East is that direction." Again, she smiled at the men. "Correct?"

"Right," said the beefy guy, settling back down, giving Tony one last dirty look.

"What street are we looking for?" Faith asked.

"Follow the main road to the other side of town. You'll see the park in about a mile," said the service attendant.

"Thanks so much."

Faith dragged Tony outside, which he really didn't mind, enjoying the feel of her soft hand grasping his own.

"This isn't exactly the time for a fight, Tony."

"They were jerks," he said in his own defense, his thumb rubbing the back of her knuckles.

She looked annoyed, but whether at the comment or his intimate touch, he wasn't sure. She didn't pull her hand free.

"Maybe they were jerks," she admitted. "But you weren't much better. It's not a good idea to come into a strange town and try to push your weight around."

He opened the door for her, then climbed into the car himself. "I was only asking a simple question."

"It was the way you asked, not what you asked. I know you're uptight, but you could try to understand. Some people, the ones who aren't so open-minded, will distrust you on your accent alone."

Amazed, he realized he was allowing her to lecture him. And it didn't even bother him. "They don't like outsiders, huh?" He pulled out onto the highway. "Kind of reminds me of the punks in my old neighborhood fighting with each other."

"About what?"

"Who knows? There were all these different ethnic groups and everybody was suspicious of each other."

Though there had also been a camaraderie of sorts within each ethnic group itself. After hearing about country customs regarding disasters and funerals, Tony had remembered a big Italian wake he'd attended where neighbors and relatives had supplied all the food.

But he had no more time for musing about the past. He spotted the trailer park up ahead. Entering the gate, he only drove around for a minute before noticing the name Hobson scrawled on a mailbox. Pulse picking up, he turned the Porsche, nearly crashing into the mailbox pole.

Faith jerked forward. "Whew. Glad I'm wearing a seat belt."

Tony was immediately concerned. "Are you okay?" He touched her shoulder and brushed back her hair. He hadn't meant to be reckless.

His gesture made her blush as she unfastened the seat belt and started to get out of the car. He smiled, liking the way he could get her all excited.

"I'm fine."

She sure was.

And she waited until he joined her to walk to the beat-up-looking trailer. A woman with dark hair lopped into a messy ponytail was already standing at the open door, a small child in her arms. Another kid clutched her blue-jeaned leg.

"Mrs. Hobson?" queried Tony.

"Yeah."

"We're looking for your husband, Zak."

She backed up, acting like she wanted to close the trailer door. "I'm not responsible for his debts."

"This isn't about debts."

The woman came forward again. Her face was sullen and her skin looked sallow against her obviously dyed black hair.

"Then what do you want?" She added, "And Zak is my ex-husband, anyway, thank God."

Tony glanced around. "He doesn't live here?"

Meantime, Naomi Hobson looked both him and Faith over, no doubt trying to ascertain who they really were. Faith hung back, letting Tony ask the questions this time. He decided to use his own approach to psychology. Naomi

Hobson looked like she could use some supportive sympathy.

"Went off and left you with the kids, huh?"

"Sure did." Naomi adjusted the child on her hip. "Haven't lived with Zak for years. Haven't even seen him very often, the dirty, no-good bum. He owes me a lot of child support."

"You never see him at all?"

"I only hear about him. If I saw him face-to-face, he knows I'd hit him up for money. I've got three mouths to feed, and food stamps only go so far. Some kinda man, huh?"

"Yeah, some kind of man," agreed Tony. "If I had kids, I'd never go off and leave them."

Which was the honest truth. He'd had the experience of being fatherless.

"Has Zak done something wrong?" Naomi's expression seemed slyly interested. "You aren't the police, are you?"

Tony had to be honest. "No."

The woman laughed. "Too bad—the creep deserves to be arrested. He hangs out with some guys who've served time in the pen. I figured they'd be up to no good and get caught one of these days."

Tony gazed down at the little kid who was looking soulfully up at him. "Do they hang out in any particular place?"

"There's a bar in Grundyville, some dive called the Red Devil. Zak is a devil all right."

"Grundyville?"

"It's north of here," said Faith, finally joining the conversation.

Tony pulled some bills from his pocket and handed them to Naomi, who took the money eagerly.

"What's this for?"

"Your trouble." He felt for her. Maybe she caused some of her own problems, but she was in a bad situation.

"Thanks." Naomi was all smiles. "I wish I could tell you for certain where Zak might be staying. Like I said, he deserves to get caught."

Tony went back to the car with Faith, figuring she'd get all mushy about his gesture and make him feel uncomfortable. "Better not tell me I'm nice."

"I'm not saying a word."

But he heard a softness in her voice that hadn't been there earlier. He jumped into the car, started it and backed up. "Have you figured out our strategy? The fastest back roads to Grundyville?" With only a little surprise, he realized he was depending on her.

She already had the map out and pointed to it. "We should go this way."

They passed a small store on the way to their gravel-road turnoff, and Tony became curious about the day's newspapers. "I wonder if there's any more articles about T.H."

"They wouldn't have Chicago papers here."

But they parked, and he quickly picked up a Des Moines *Tribune*. As he drove, Faith found a small article about the kidnapped horse on the inner pages.

"So far, so good. At least no one's saying anything happened to him," said Tony, speeding along as usual. When a tractor and a wagon pulled out from a lane on the side, forcing him to brake sharply, he cursed, but tried not to get too upset. "Guess I should chill out. It's not like Zak Hobson'll be sitting around in the Red Devil waiting for us to find him."

"But we're getting closer."

Tony hoped so, actually believed it in his gut. The same way he'd known Faith would be good to bring along. For nearly two days, she'd been his anchor, his support . . . and more.

The tractor finally got out of the way, and Tony took off with a spray of rock.

"Describe Zak Hobson again."

"Short red hair, freckles, high cheekbones, a big nose, a mean expression." Then she asked, "What do you plan to do if you see him?"

"*Plan* to do or *want* to do?"

"Plan. We have to be careful. We need to find T.H. Not to mention that Hobson is probably dangerous, very likely armed. People often carry shotguns in the country."

"If he has a gun, I'll stick it down his throat."

"Come on." Her voice had a little worrisome tone that turned him on. "I know you're tough, but you don't need to be ridiculous."

"Tough? I thought you said I was mush inside."

"Only a little mushy. You have a heart—that's all I meant."

"I don't have a heart for a guy like Hobson."

Though he had plenty of heart for a woman like her. She had guts and tenacity, had refused to leave him, even when he'd given her the chance. Instinctively, he knew he could trust her. Lady luck must have been smiling on him the day Faith Murray showed up, for she was the type to stick with a man, even if he had to face the devil himself.

A big, ugly face with horns and a goatee had been painted on the single, narrow window of the Red Devil Bar.

"What a sleazy-looking place," said Faith, though she thought it was probably a perfect hangout for Zak Hobson.

They sat in the Porsche, parked diagonally a few slots away on the small-town street. Tony placed his hand on the door handle.

"You're not going in there, are you? Hobson will recognize you. He must know you from the backstretch."

"I'll be careful. I wanna look around."

"Then why don't you let me go inside? Hobson surely wouldn't remember me." She drew back her hair and pulled a scarf from her purse. "And I can put this on. He won't recognize me at all."

Tony smiled crookedly. "You're willing to do anything to try to stop me from sticking his gun down his throat, huh?"

"I'm trying to avoid arousing too much suspicion."

"Okay, go."

But no one need have worried. The Red Devil was almost deserted as Faith went inside. A man sat at the bar nursing a beer. He stared at her, as did the bartender. For a moment, she considered asking about Hobson, then decided against it. In his own territory, the man's friends could be anyone, and they wouldn't give him up.

Sighting a sign for rest rooms at the back of the place, Faith headed there, passing a couple in a booth. They were so busy making out, they didn't notice her. Faith gazed at them more closely when she came out of the bathroom, then stopped at a cooler full of beer and soda. She took out a cola and paid the bartender before leaving.

Tony was tapping his fingers on the side of the Porsche and looking tense as she approached.

"I hope Zak Hobson doesn't know what kind of car you have," she remarked, climbing inside.

"Me, too. He's not inside the bar at the moment, I assume."

She shook her head. "Only some big guy chugging a beer and a couple in a booth."

He continued tapping his fingers, but some of the tension seemed to leave him.

"But that doesn't mean Hobson won't show up, maybe even tonight," she told him. "I'm sure the evening will be busier. People usually work day hours in the country, even more so than in the city."

"What are these people doing, then—taking a coffee break?"

"I don't know about the beer guy's story, but the couple was having a hot rendezvous."

"Yeah?" He turned his gaze on her, eyes hidden behind his sunglasses. "Sounds like fun."

A thrill shot through Faith. She was certain he was thinking of the way they'd made out the night before. Suddenly she wished she had more of a wardrobe with her, as well as a blow dryer. She might be clean, but she hadn't been able to style her hair after showering, and her sweatshirt and jeans were beginning to feel groady.

His gaze was disconcerting as he asked, "Can I have some soda?"

"Sure." She handed the cola to him. "Sorry, I probably should have gotten two."

"Sharing is okay—I don't have any deadly diseases."

She watched him drink, watched his lips press against the soda can's rim. Those lips had covered hers last night. Their tongues had touched. She'd run her fingers through that crisp, dark hair. The silver strands at his temples added a fascinating maturity to his rugged face, she decided, suddenly too warm for comfort.

"So, you don't have a boyfriend at the moment, hmm?"

She nearly jumped out of her skin, wondering if he could read her mind. "I already told you I don't, no."

"Uh-uh, you said you didn't have enough time for dating." He raised a brow. "But I think you'd make time for a guy if you found the right one. I think you're a passionate woman."

Passionate? Again she felt a thrill. "I don't know about that." She wasn't the type of woman who always had a man to warm her bed, that was for certain.

"*I* know," Tony said. "You have powerful feelings."

He handed the soda back to her, allowing his fingers to linger against hers. He had strong hands, needed strength to handle spirited, thousand-pound horses.

"How come you haven't found the right man?" he asked. "You must not have been looking too hard. Or are you waiting for that cowboy?"

"I'm not likely to find a cowboy in a city like Chicago."

"Then maybe you should move to Denver." He glanced out at the street, then back to her. "How come you like cowboys, anyway?"

How come he was asking so many questions? And such personal ones. Faith shifted uncomfortably, hoping she could avoid answering, but he kept waiting.

"Cowboys have always appealed to me, that's all," she finally said. "Maybe because they're strong, outdoorsy, independent." She could add that a cowboy was also a horseman, but figured Tony could apply the description to himself. She didn't want to add to his already swelled head. "You don't have to be concerned about my love life, okay?" She was more embarrassed than annoyed. "I can take care of myself."

"You're not doing such a hot job. How old did you say you were? Twenty-eight?"

She tried to laugh. "Are you implying I'm an old maid? That's outmoded thinking."

"I didn't say any such thing. But you must not have much going on in your life if you were willing to take off for parts unknown with a stranger."

Now that remark bothered her. Though she wasn't about to explain, once again, that she cared about T.H., that coming along with Tony was a spur-of-the-moment decision. Not to mention that she had been working and going to school for so long that she felt imprisoned by her own schedule . . . and, yes, a bit bored. She was surprised at the hunger for excitement she'd found reawakening within herself over the past couple of days.

"Did I hurt your feelings?" Once more, he gazed at her deeply, eyes barely visible behind the shades.

He'd touched her, but she wasn't about to admit it. She said huffily, "You don't understand me well enough to really hurt me."

He winced. "Ouch, there's that mouth again. You can be nasty when you want to be."

"Only when someone is annoying me. You're obviously spoiling for a fight, picking at me this way."

"A little wrestling wouldn't be a bad idea."

The very idea of which titillated her. "We'd have a difficult time wrestling in a two-seater like this."

"The seats go back some if you hit the right button—want to try?"

She stilled the thrill that immediately jumped through her. "Sure. Wouldn't that be the perfect way to keep watch for Zak Hobson?"

He grinned. "Hey, I'm only joking." He reached for the can of soda, again letting his fingers linger.

Until her skin prickled, making her jerk away. "What got you into this lover-boy mode all of a sudden, anyway?" What was good for the goose was good for the gander, she decided. Tony could use a little shaking up himself. "Are your hormones kicking up? Has it been too long a time since you had an evening out with the ladies?" Let *him* answer some personal questions for a change.

"I've had some evenings out with a lady. She gave me some pretty hot kisses, too."

He'd turned the conversation right back to her!

Face warm, she murmured, "That just happened.... I was feeling emotional." Why did he insist on making her uncomfortable? "Both of us were upset."

"Sure, you're not attracted to me at all."

"I told you you're attractive. I didn't deny it."

"Even if I don't wear a Stetson and Western boots?" He added, "I may not be a cowboy, but I have a horse."

"*Had* a horse. The best horse in the U.S., until someone stole him."

Which made Tony sober. Both of them stared at the bar. As they did so, the young couple who'd been inside came out with their arms wrapped around each other. Laughing, the man pushed his girlfriend up against the car and kissed her heatedly.

"They're head over heels, all right," said Tony, finishing off the can of soda.

"In love?"

"Or lust." Then he asked, "Have you ever been in love?"

Now, this was too much. "Have you?"

"Yeah."

"You loved your ex-wife?"

"Her, too."

"Too? Surely you're not going to claim you fell in love with every woman you've ever gone out with."

"Not anymore. When I was young, I thought I was in love every other week." He glanced at the romantic couple, who were still embracing. "I kind of miss that—but it would be difficult to pull off now, knowing what I do."

"What's that?"

"Love is a mess."

She should have known his cynicism would kick in, but he always had a good reason. "You must have had a bitter divorce."

"And a bitter marriage to boot. My wife never wanted me for myself. She was more interested in money and connections. She thought I was going up in the world."

"Which you did."

"Eventually, but not fast enough for her. She was long gone by the time T.H. won the Kentucky Derby."

Suddenly he crushed the empty soda can, a gesture Faith hated.

"Love can be a real drag."

"Especially if a person is as cynical and negative as you."

"Negative?" He raised his brows. "You should know."

She frowned. "What are you talking about?"

"You obviously don't believe in much yourself or you wouldn't have been stuck in a situation you wanted to run away from...and you wouldn't still be alone. You never answered my question about being in love, but I bet the answer is no."

"That's not true," Faith said, knowing she sounded far more defensive than she wanted to. "I—I've been in love."

Sort of, she thought, maybe her last year of high school. And, well, she'd dated several guys she'd met in college classes...though she had to admit she hadn't really fancied herself in love with any of them.

"Come on, you don't want to take a chance any more than I do." He turned toward her, lounging back against the seat. "You lost too much, including your horse. You're afraid to dream anymore."

Opening her mouth to object, Faith froze when she caught a glimpse of a man going into the Red Devil. She immediately sat up straighter. "There goes a tall man with red hair."

Immediately alert, Tony sank down in his seat and peered out the window. "Where?"

"Wait until he comes out again."

It only took a few minutes. Faith gave a little cry as Zak Hobson strode out of the bar carrying a paper bag, probably a six-pack. The short sleeves of his shirt revealed his tattoo. He headed down the block.

"That's him!"

"Damn it, I'm gonna kill the jerk!"

Tony reached for the door handle, and Faith grabbed him.

"Settle down! You don't mean that," she warned, actually holding on to him to keep him in the car. "We've got to follow him and find T.H."

It was obviously all Tony could do to keep his cool. Zak Hobson disappeared around the corner of the building at the far end of the block. Tony's hand trembled slightly as he turned the key in the ignition, slowly backing out to drive down the street and around the corner. There was no one in sight.

Tony looked around, expression wild. "Okay, where the hell is he?"

"He must have gotten into a car or truck."

Though the blue pickup Faith had seen Zak in at Rolling Meadows Racecourse was nowhere to be seen. Tony took off after a brown sedan, the only vehicle that was moving anywhere. They followed it to the edge of town, Tony telling Faith to get the binoculars out of the glove compartment. When she did so, she realized neither of the sedan's occupants were Zak Hobson.

"They're an elderly couple, Tony."

Nevertheless, he stepped down on the accelerator, coming right up to tailgate the sedan before passing it with barely an inch to spare.

"Sure Hobson's not lying down in the back seat?"

"I'm sure." Just as certain as she was that the elderly couple were freaked out by Tony's bizarre driving. The man at the wheel looked wide-eyed and shaky at being dive-bombed by a black Porsche. "Let's get out of here," Faith said through her teeth.

Though she was terribly embarrassed, she put on a good front. She smiled and waved at the sedan, hoping that would make the old guy feel better. Tony sped up, easily leaving the sedan behind. A couple of miles along, he roared off onto a side road, made a wheelie of a U-turn and came to a shuddering stop.

"Damn it all, what happened to Hobson?"

Happy that both they and the car were intact, Faith took a deep breath. "He must have sneaked off somehow. Maybe he went into a house or got into another vehicle we didn't see."

"I should have gotten outta the car."

"Then he would have seen you for sure. This way, he doesn't know we're after him."

Tony glanced about. Cornfields and pastures surrounded them. A barn and a silo were visible in the distance.

"How many people are there in Iowa, anyway? I heard there were less than the whole population of Chicago. Dubuque County can't have more than a couple hundred thousand. How come we can't find this guy?"

As if a couple of hundred thousand wasn't that many. But Faith knew Tony was merely frustrated and upset.

"We did find Hobson—we just didn't catch him. Maybe he'll come back to the Red Devil tonight."

"Or maybe he won't. I don't want to wait. They've got T.H. stashed around here somewhere. How big is this damned county? Can't we drive up and down all the roads and look for that horse trailer—"

"You're talking about a lot of stock trailers. Only a person with an experienced eye would notice a strange vehicle in the neighborhood. Or a chestnut horse." She thought hard for a moment. "It would be best to keep T.H. out in the country, right?"

"As opposed to one of these two-bit towns?"

"More people would tend to notice a horse there." Even though some municipalities did allow livestock within the city limits. "An experienced eye," she mused softly. "You know, I have an idea."

Chapter Eight

A half hour later, Faith and Tony were on their way to question an old-time local farmer. Faith had phoned her uncle in Dubuque. Uncle Will had once been a stock-feed salesman who had worked the northern area of the county and who had several friendly acquaintances to recommend.

"Why didn't you call this guy before?" Tony complained.

"You're so appreciative." He just gave her a slanted look, so she explained. "Because I was afraid he'd tell my parents what I was doing, that's why." She didn't bother to hide the edge to her voice. "I thought they'd be worried about me."

"They *should* be worried about you."

Which didn't make Faith feel any better. At least her uncle had promised to keep her activities secret for the moment.

"I had to reassure Uncle Will over and over, and had to tell him about the stolen horse or he wouldn't have given me any names at all. And I had to fib about our plans for True Heart." Not that Faith hadn't been wondering about rescue plans herself—exactly what they were and how she and Tony were going to carry them out. But she guessed they should find the horse first. "I indicated I was only going along with you because I was an eyewitness, and I assured him that once I identified the thieves, you were going to send me home."

"I should send you home."

Faith hardened her jaw. "I'll go back to Chicago when *I* choose to," she said in no uncertain terms. "And you'd better respect that. You couldn't have gotten this far without me." Again, she was irritated because he didn't seem to realize he should be grateful.

Instead, he kept his eyes on the road, his expression impassive. "Who's this Sawyer guy again?"

"A farmer who's been living in this area all his life. My uncle says the man is outgoing and knows everyone in the vicinity."

"And what's he gonna think about us?"

"I have no idea—my uncle phoned him and said I'd be visiting."

"I suppose we'll have to tell him the truth about T.H."

"Well, you won't have to worry about Myron Sawyer calling in the highway patrol or the FBI. My uncle's the old-fashioned, independent type of cuss who distrusts the government and anybody who works for it, and his friends are of the same opinion."

"Old-fashioned and independent, huh? Sounds like a dying breed."

"Along with the small towns, I'm afraid." Faith glanced out at the fields as they passed. "Huge chain stores are replacing small, individually owned ones. Someday the area will probably be loaded with corporate farms, too." She sighed. "I guess I'm not always happy with the way the world is changing." Though she'd tried to adjust.

"If they could talk, horses would agree." Tony sounded reflective. "Technology pretty much ended their usefulness. Racing is one of the few jobs they can still get."

Faith hadn't thought of it like that.

"I bet there aren't many real cowboys left, either," Tony said. "The independent type of hombre who rides into town on his own, keeps his own counsel. Maybe you'd better think about going out West and catching one as soon as you get the chance."

She gave him an intense look, wondering why he'd brought up the subject now. "I wasn't serious about wanting a cowboy. That was only a daydream."

A daydream Tony was constantly reminding her about. Not that Faith hadn't been inclined to muse on fantasies and dreams throughout this trip, anyway, partially because they were always on the move and never had enough sleep. Added to that, it truly was an incredible adventure.

Though one for which she prayed there'd be a good ending.

Time was running out for T.H. Faith only hoped that Myron Sawyer would be able to help them.

A few minutes later she anxiously looked for the farmer as Tony pulled into the Sawyers' driveway. But no one was waiting for them on the front porch of the neat white farmhouse. An old truck sat under a copse of fir trees nearby and a collie mix ran out to bark at the Porsche.

A white-haired woman also came past the house's screen door to stare at them and call off the dog. "Don't worry about him—he's harmless." She looked Tony up and down as the two approached, but she spoke to Faith. "Are you Will Murray's niece?"

"Sure am." Faith smiled and offered her hand. "I'm Faith, and this is Tony."

Mrs. Sawyer seemed friendly enough. "Well, it's Myron you want to talk to, right? He didn't tell me all the details, but he said you were searching for someone." She gestured. "He's down by the barn finishing the chores."

Faith and Tony headed in that direction, the farm dog ambling behind them.

"Chores?" Tony queried, taking off his sunglasses and sticking them in his shirt pocket. "You mean like taking care of animals?"

"Right. It's late afternoon. You always check on feed and water, milk the cows if you have any, look the livestock over before dark."

"You used to do all that?"

"I helped."

"A regular farmer's daughter, huh?" His voice was low and gravelly.

"You make that sound like I was part of an off-color joke."

"You? Mary Poppins, an off-color joke?" Still, his grin seemed a tad lecherous—as if he might be imagining her naked in a hayloft.

A hayloft? Good heavens!

Faith realized she had no trouble also imagining Tony unclothed and embracing her in the hay. Growing warm all over, goose bumps rising on her neck and arms, she told herself all this attraction stuff was at least adding some comic relief to an intense situation. Their emotions heightened, they could easily swing from passionately serious to fervently funny. That's why they'd gotten into that ridiculous discussion earlier about love and boyfriends and cowboys. That's why they'd gotten into a clinch the night before.

Wasn't it?

Her speculations ended as they neared the lots and the barn. Some holstein feeder calves milled about in the enclosure on one side of the building. On the other, she spotted Myron Sawyer carrying two heavy buckets. Several horses stood about in the lot—a big, stocky workhorse, a couple of Shetland ponies, a brown-and-white paint and a tall bay.

"Horses." Tony didn't hesitate opening the gate to the lot and going inside, Faith beside him. "Need some help?"

"Sure," said Sawyer, a big, seventyish man with slightly stooped shoulders. "These hayburners are a lot of work. And they eat me out of house and home."

Tony took one of the buckets and dumped it in the trough Sawyer indicated. "Since they cost so much, how come you keep so many?"

"Aw, I like having horses around. Always did. Guess they remind me of my daddy's team—Maud and Bess—and those fields we used to plow together." Sawyer gestured toward the shaggy Shetland ponies. "Some neighbors dumped those two on me. Said I either had to take them or they were going to the glue factory."

"I'm sure glad you like horses, Mr. Sawyer." Faith followed the two men to the other side of the lot where Tony helped the farmer with a rusty water pump. "Because that's why we're here."

"Oh?" Sawyer looked interested.

"I'm Faith Murray, Will's niece. This is Tony D'Angelo, the trainer of True Heart, who won the Kentucky Derby this year. He's been kidnapped."

"Kidnapped? The horse?"

"Yes, and we have reason to believe he's being held in this vicinity," Faith went on. "We saw one of the thieves in Grundyville just a while ago, the same guy who was driving a pickup and horse trailer out of Rolling Meadows Racecourse the day that True Heart was stolen."

"The thieves are asking for a ransom of two million," Tony added. "If they don't get it and fast, they're gonna kill my buddy."

Myron Sawyer had a few sparse gray hairs sticking out from under his billed cap, but his eyebrows were thick and black. Those brows rose higher and higher as he grasped all the details. "Horse thieves! Damn, in this day and age? Did you notify the cops?"

Faith exchanged glances with Tony.

"Uh, well, that's kind of a problem," he began.

"A big problem. *We're* wanted by the police," Faith told Sawyer. "Because the theft was an inside job. We think one or both of True Heart's owners are involved. As soon as we left Chicago to find the horse, someone put warrants out on us."

Sawyer simply nodded. "What are these people up to—collecting insurance?"

"Something like that," said Tony. "But I don't care who's involved or what they want, T.H. doesn't deserve to die for somebody else's problems or greed. That colt ran his heart out for me, for them, for everyone who was watching the race. You should have seen him flying down the stretch at Churchill Downs. He was giving it his all."

Again, Sawyer nodded. "I did see him. I always watch the Kentucky Derby on TV, have watched it for years." He looped his thumbs in the straps of his striped overalls, his thick eyebrows pulling into a single line of a scowl. "So what're we going to do?"

"We?" repeated Tony.

"Think I'll get my shotguns out and clean them," grumbled Sawyer. "We've got some vermin to shoot."

Tony could hardly believe his ears. Myron Sawyer, a man who didn't even know him, was offering to join up for T.H.'s rescue!

"A'course, I'm going to have to make a slew of phone calls first," Sawyer went on. "We've got to find out where they're hiding the horse."

"I'd sincerely appreciate that," Tony told him. "But forget about the shotguns, okay? I don't want anyone else in danger."

Sawyer snorted. "Danger, hell! I can get a dozen good old boys together in less than an hour. We can make Swiss cheese out of them thieves ... or else hang 'em from a big tree. Your choice."

Tony was touched by Sawyer's genuine outrage, but he continued to try to dissuade the man. "I don't think the authorities would appreciate that kind of action."

"Authorities?" Sawyer raised his voice. "What are they doing to protect us little guys, the average American? Hell, half the time criminals are getting off scot-free, just the same as politicians, and big companies take turns stealing money from the public like a pack of bandits. We need to take some action ourselves."

Geez, if he didn't watch out, Tony figured he'd be heading up a throng of well-meaning vigilantes. He glanced at Faith and hoped she understood his silent plea.

She touched the older man's arm, gazed up at him with big, soft eyes. "Please, Mr. Sawyer. We don't want a bloodbath. We don't even want any violence. We just want to get the horse back, so he'll be safe. No one needs to get hurt, and we would feel especially terrible if that person were someone like you. Think about your wife and your children and grandchildren."

Sawyer frowned. "Well..."

"I'm sure we can find other ways you can help us," Tony assured him. "For one thing, you know the people to call."

Sawyer nodded.

Obviously trying to keep the man thinking along the same lines, Faith detailed a description of the dark blue pickup, the trailer, the license plate and Zak Hobson. Soon they were all moving toward the house.

Once inside, Sawyer gave his wife a short explanation and sat down to use the phone. In the middle of putting food on the table, Mrs. Sawyer insisted Tony and Faith have some supper.

Tony's mouth watered at the sight of a roast, mashed potatoes, homemade biscuits and corn on the cob. His stomach rumbled. They had forgotten to pick up some lunch.

But he said, "We don't want to be any trouble."

"Don't worry, there's more here than Myron and I can eat by ourselves. And dig in right away. You don't have to wait for my husband to come to the table."

"We certainly appreciate your hospitality," said Faith, helping herself to an ear of corn.

That's all it took for Tony to fill his plate.

Mrs. Sawyer adjusted her silver-rimmed glasses. "You two look pretty tired and hungry."

"No wonder, we've been trying to chase someone down for two days," Tony said.

He glanced toward Sawyer and the phone conversation when he heard something about a corporation that had bought up some land nearby. But Sawyer soon hung up on that call and started making another. Eagerly awaiting any news, Tony was almost done eating when the man finally came to the table. He chewed on a bite of his third buttered biscuit.

"Well, your horse is in this neighborhood, all right," said the farmer.

Tony choked, the biscuit sticking in his throat.

Sawyer slapped him on the back, hard. "Whoa, don't kill yourself."

Tony motioned that he was okay, though he coughed some more, tears coming to his eyes. Finally he found his voice. "Where? When did they see him?"

"This very morning a friend of mine saw a fine-looking red horse grazing on the old Hollandorf place . . . a deserted farm," Sawyer explained. "Neither the land nor the buildings have been used for years and years."

"How far away?"

"A couple of miles."

"My God, that close!"

Tony started to get up, but Sawyer placed a big hand on his shoulder and pushed him back down. He was strong for seventy. "You'd better think about your strategy, boy, before you go off like a firecracker. My friend also seen a blue pickup and a couple of men hanging around the place."

"And one of those men has red hair, I bet," put in Faith.

"He didn't say anything about hair color," Sawyer said. "Now how are you going to go about this thing—if you aren't going to take advantage of the posse I could raise?"

"No posse." Tony shook his head adamantly. "Can you give me the lay of the land? Draw a rough map?"

"That'll be no problem."

"And I noticed that truck you've got parked out there. Can I buy it from you?" Though how he was going to get the cash at this moment, Tony wasn't sure.

"You can't buy that truck."

Tony's heart sank.

"But you can use it . . . for free. You won't be able to take your car with you, anyway, unless you want to be picked up by the state patrol. You were mighty lucky to have escaped them so far with that fancy job you're driving."

"I can leave the Porsche as collateral," Tony offered, uncomfortable with the man's generosity. After all, Sawyer didn't owe him anything.

But the older man waved his offer away. "I'll be happy to park the car in a shed until you come back for it. But not as collateral. That truck is twenty years old and still running, which is about all it has going for it. If anything happens to it, I don't care."

Tony didn't know what to say. Some biscuit stuck in his throat. "That's kind of you."

"It's the least I can do. I know you must be a decent man—if his niece is anything like Will Murray, she's the salt of the earth and wouldn't take up with a joker or a fool."

She wouldn't? Tony thought, sneaking a glance at Faith. She must have detected things in him that very few others had. Not that he was dishonest or violent—nothing like that. Was this connection thing they had growing on her, too?

"You know, there's something strange about that farm those thieves are using," Sawyer went on.

Which interrupted Tony's thoughts. "What's that?"

"It was bought by some company years back and left to lie fallow."

"A company?"

"Some kind of plastics manufacturer. Isn't that odd?"

"Plastics?" That rang a bell. "Anybody know the company's name? Not G.B.L. Plastics?"

"I believe that's it." Mrs. Sawyer said, joining in the conversation. "That's what one of the ladies in my card club said."

Tony hardened his jaw. "George."

Faith met his gaze.

"G.B.L. Plastics is George Langley's company," Tony told Sawyer. "He's one of T.H.'s owners. And maybe I was wrong, maybe the other owner is innocent." After all, it was George's wife who never had enough houses; it was George who was always griping about how much money his horses made. "Still, it's terrible to think about either way. You don't like to believe that anyone is so unprincipled."

"Can you prove all this?" asked Sawyer.

"I'm certain I can. With you and your friends . . . and Faith willing to testify about the trailer and the land ownership."

Mrs. Sawyer smiled. "We'll do whatever we can."

"But first we have to get the colt away from them." This time, Sawyer didn't push Tony back down when he rose from the table. "Can I take a look at that truck?"

"Sure, and then I'll draw you a map. Are you going over there tonight?"

"I think it's best. But I may have to wait until the wee hours to catch them off guard. I'll have to stake out the place."

"Then you'll need some blankets and some food," said Mrs. Sawyer, also rising from the table. "I'll pack it up."

Faith followed her to help. "We don't know how to thank you. This is very generous."

"Yeah," agreed Tony. "We're gonna pay you back some way, no matter what you say."

"Forget about it," growled Sawyer. "I'll be paid when I see that horse run another race."

"Then you're gonna be watching him from box seats." Tony shook the man's hand. "That's the least I can do."

Though at the moment, to Tony, the mere thought of seeing T.H. alive was more exciting than setting up another race. But he wished the horse would run again and that he would win, if only to make Sawyer happy. The farmer was a kind old soul, as well as a brave, independent cuss. He had heart.

Heart. Tony watched Faith helping Mrs. Sawyer pack some food. Faith had stood beside him, had just about held his hand ever since T.H. had been stolen and he'd gotten over the mistake of thinking her involved with the deed. He wasn't sure why he had so much trouble admitting it openly, but he didn't know what he would have done without her. Sometimes he couldn't conceive of how he'd do without her in the future.

The future? He was letting his feelings get a bit out of hand. But then, the high-stakes situation was getting to him, and might be getting to Faith, as well. Perhaps that's why she was being so adamant about staying with him, so fearless about backing him up and rescuing the horse.

Maybe he should be concerned for her emotional safety, as well as the threat of physical danger.

At last, they'd found T.H.!

Pulse racing, Faith helped ready the truck, the rear of which was a latticework stock hauler with a half gate across the back that could be lowered to use as a ramp. Tony loaded a couple of canvas bags from his car, then spread straw over the floor. Myron Sawyer contributed a bucket, some rope and a bale of hay, while his wife threw in some blankets, a bag of sandwiches and a big thermos of iced tea. The farmer also insisted they fill up the vehicle from the gasoline tank he kept for tractors near the barn. As they did so, the men drew off to talk, stopping abruptly when Faith seemed to be listening.

Which worried her, caused her to fear she'd be ordered to stay behind at the farm. But Tony made no objection when she climbed into the truck's passenger seat. Small binoculars hanging about his neck, he took off with a grinding of gears. Nearly an hour after they'd eaten, the sun sank, starting to gray the land around them with twilight.

"The Hollandorf place is bordered by a cornfield, right?" At least, that's what Faith had understood. "We should sneak up to the farm's fence line by walking down a corn row. Since it's a good year for crops, the stalks will be tall enough to offer cover."

"That's what Sawyer suggested." Tony was driving along as swiftly as the grumbling old truck would allow. He frowned, as if he were mulling something over in his mind. "Look, we need to talk."

Great, here it came. "Don't tell me I can't come along with you. It's a little late now, don't you think?"

"I'm not saying you can't stay with the truck. But it'll be me who sneaks up on the men and gets T.H."

"While I back you up."

"No." The scar darkened above his brow.

"Yes."

He let out a big sigh. "You're too damned stubborn, Faith. Think about your parents. And the other people who love you—brothers, sisters?"

"So I have a brother." Not that he had anything to do with this decision. "You know, you're catching on, Tony. You're using the same diplomatic prattle I employed with Sawyer."

"But you were right. You appealed to his heart. And I'm appealing to yours. You've got too much going for you to put yourself in danger."

"And what about you? Think you could get yourself killed and nobody would notice?" Her mind raced, searching for the right thing to say. "If nothing else, you're one of the most famous Thoroughbred trainers in the country."

"At the moment. But newspapers and fans will forget about me if I don't have another big winner next year. They only care about famous races and important stories."

"Surely there are other people who would miss you."

His smile was more ironic than anything. "To tell you the truth, I'm not sure who that would be. I've got some friends who would go so far as to say they like me, but I can count those guys on less than five fingers. While you... Well, even your crazy neighbor is worried about you."

Faith had told him how Audra had offered to come to Iowa to get her. She swallowed. "I would miss you, Tony. I care."

And she meant that, had seen the depth of emotion in this man, the warm heart he tried to hide from other people. She'd seen him furtively deposit money in a donation box and hand more over to a hard-drinking divorcée with three children and a no-good husband. She'd seen the surprised gratefulness in his eyes when Myron Sawyer had befriended him.

Now Tony's expression became oddly sober. "Don't waste your feelings on me, Faith."

Feelings? "I didn't say I loved you."

But she did love him, Faith realized with shock, even as she attempted to deny it. And she didn't just love Tony as a friend, she was *in love* with him. She wondered if he could read the fact in her expression, if her new consciousness was transparent. But if he should guess how she felt, she wasn't afraid. Suddenly life had taken on a new dimension—something powerful and beautiful had opened up inside her.

"I'm coming with you—flood, fire or bullets," she told him fervently, pointing to the cornfield up ahead. "Isn't that the spot Sawyer mentioned? With the gate on one side of the road and the pullover for the truck on the other?"

Tony sighed again, but slowed to take a look. He braked the truck to a creaking stop, turned down a dirt incline and into the shelter of some trees.

"Hope no one pays much attention to this beater while we're figuring out how to capture T.H. and lead him back."

We. She smiled. "So you're accepting my company."

"I don't like endangering you, but I can't do much about it, unless I get physical, tie you up again."

"Not to mention that you really need another pair of hands and eyes. You can't do everything alone."

But as she'd expected, Tony didn't respond to that. He remained silent as they got out and took some things from the back—a blanket, the bag of food, the thermos, the rope. Tony rummaged in one of the canvas bags he'd taken from his trunk, withdrawing a long, thin object.

Faith felt a chill. "A gun?"

"Nah, I hate guns." Slinging the rope over one shoulder, he showed her a baseball bat and swung it around. "Something like this used to do fine in my old neighborhood. You can even take an armed man if you know how to use it."

Armed men. Thinking about the real threat of bullets, Faith swiped at the chills pebbling her arms. This was no daydream. But she refused to have second thoughts.

"At least promise me you'll follow my directions," Tony urged. "I've had more experience with punks than you."

"I promise." She would give him that.

Adjusting the blanket, the bag of food and the thermos, she headed for the cornfield. Tony opened the gate, then fastened it behind them. They followed a narrow trough between the rows and walked into the tall corn. Planted closely to get the most yield, the forest of stalks offered rough going. Faith stumbled a couple of times over clods of soil. Gusts of restless wind muffled their footsteps with the crackling of drying leaves.

They slowed as they neared the fence bordering the weed-choked, deserted farm. An old barbed-wire fence sagged between the properties.

Faith stepped closer and whispered. "The fence posts are rotten. We can pull the wire down and hold it with our feet to get through."

Tony stiffened as he gazed beyond the fence toward a barn and some sheds gray with age. "Hit the dust. I caught some movement."

Dropping what she carried, Faith followed Tony's lead and fell to the ground. Then they crept forward on their stomachs, halting at the narrow, grassy border near the fence. The barn and sheds were some distance away, as were a couple of moving figures. One of them had four legs and a chestnut coat that glimmered red in the dying light. T.H.! Faith's heart beat faster.

Tony raised the small binoculars.

"Is he okay?"

"He's lost weight," Tony said, sounding unhappy. "Some guy is grazing him, but they obviously haven't been feeding him well. He's really chomping on those grass blades."

She placed a gentle, sympathetic hand on Tony's shoulder. "How's his leg?"

"I can't tell for sure . . . but he's not favoring it." He adjusted the binoculars. "It doesn't look bad at all."

"Is that strange?"

"Considering they haven't been doing anything for him—he's not even wearing standing bandages. Maybe there's a God in heaven and all my buddy needed was some rest." Then he lowered his voice. "Here comes Zak Hobson."

"Can I look?" She took the binoculars, moving them from T.H. and the rough-looking, mustached man who held him, to a sudden, close-up view of the mean, freckled face of the man who'd been driving the pickup at the racetrack. She nearly jumped when his narrow eyes seemed to slide in her direction, but she was sure he couldn't spot either her or Tony. "That's Hobson, all right. And he's carrying a gun."

"I noticed. An automatic."

As she handed the binoculars back, the two men and the horse headed toward the old barn. Soon they disappeared around the corner.

"So what kind of move do you have in mind?"

"For one, we'll have to wait until those two are separated. No doubt the other guy has a gun, too." Tony added worriedly, "We can't even be sure there's only two men. And it's gonna be dark soon. I wish we'd gotten here earlier."

Again, she placed a hand on his shoulder, meaning to comfort him. "At least we got here, period."

"Asking me to be grateful to you again?"

"I didn't say that."

"But you meant it." He removed her hand, holding it as he faced her. "Sorry, but there's something you should know about me and women, Faith. For sure you should know it before you get your feelings all messed up."

Chapter Nine

"Don't worry about my feelings, Tony. I can take care of them myself."

He had trouble believing that. He'd felt the connection between them growing the past two days, becoming a bond so intense and magnetic, he was certain he could hone in on her in the dark. She'd gotten him thinking and talking about issues he usually avoided, had made him achingly aware of her every gesture and movement. Even now, electricity seemed to flow between them via their entwined fingers. They communicated without words. With a sigh, he let go, gently placing her hand beside her hip on the grass.

"I'm no good for you, Faith. Either I use a woman or she uses me. That's not because I like it that way—it just is." And it was the only way he could handle being close to someone, he knew, suddenly growing uncomfortable with what had until now been perfectly acceptable.

"And you think you've used me to find True Heart?"

"I'm not talking about T.H." He hesitated, seeking the right words, wanting to be straight without hurting Faith's feelings. "I'm talking about love, commitment...even sex."

"None of which I've asked you for."

But he could sense deep feelings in her, could sense them in himself. "You're saying you're not hung up on me in any way?"

"Why do you care? Aren't you supposed to be the heart-breaking playboy type?" she asked flippantly.

He chose to be truthful. "My not getting too involved with any one woman serves a purpose."

"Oh?"

"Protection. The one relationship I really cared about blew up in my face. I figured if I didn't get too close, that couldn't happen again."

"Your ex-wife really hurt you."

"She hurt me bad. I tried to forget her by going out with every woman who gave me the eye. It hasn't been a real satisfying deal," he admitted.

Uncertain why he was making such a big confession, he rolled over to gaze up at the sky. Stars already glittered in the quickly darkening expanse.

"I got the reputation of being a womanizer at the track," he went on. "I guess it was easier to go along with the gossip than buck it."

"Don't you mean it was easier on you?" Faith asked softly. "By feeding the gossip mongers, you were protecting yourself from getting involved with anyone who might truly and deeply care. You figure your reputation will drive that kind away."

Exactly what he'd hoped to do with Faith. He frowned, again uncomfortable. "You've taken some psychology classes along with business, right?"

"It doesn't take an expert to know that love is scary. It can hurt you ... as you've learned." She paused. "But love can also free you if you let it, give you an experience you can't get from anything else."

She was speaking from experience, he knew, and he didn't think that came from any man she'd been involved with in the past. That she might be speaking of him both thrilled him and made his mouth go dry.

"You were right about my being cynical beneath my Mary Poppins facade," she admitted. "Not to mention downright cowardly. I didn't have the nerve to dream, much less think about what I really wanted in life."

"And you're gonna change now, I hope."

"I'm going to examine other options." She, too, turned over to gaze up at the stars. "And I want you to know that you helped me rethink my life—you and your raw courage and your toughness. You ran away from home and faced the world on your own. You dealt with people from all levels of society, along with racing's ups and downs. And when someone stole the horse you loved the most, you set out after them with nothing but bulldog determination and a baseball bat. You've really got guts."

Though Faith herself had had a whole lot to do with this journey, Tony thought. Whatever courage he had seemed to be amplified by her very presence. He only wished he could tell her that. But if he opened up, if he let the hidden words spill out, he'd put them both in a sticky situation.

Still, devil on his shoulder, he felt compelled to ask, "You're not in love with me, huh?"

A few long heartbeats passed.

"I love you," she said finally, softly. "But you don't have to worry about telling me that you love me in return. I feel so good, so warm and beautiful inside that I'll be fine no matter what."

He swallowed, a lump in his throat. "You deserve to be loved back, Faith." And to be offered his heart and soul. She also deserved to live a happy, settled life, not the gypsy existence of moving from racetrack to racetrack. "This trip might have been an adventure, but not the kind that happens everyday. Everything seems more intense and important, but it won't last."

"I'm aware of that, but I don't want to lose what I've found. I came back to Iowa to get *my* horse... really my courage and my heart. The past couple of days have put a new spin on everything for me."

"How's that?"

"I'll finish my degree, but I figure I don't have to work for a big corporation. And I probably will move away from the city, to a nice suburb with lots of trees and grass. Someday I'm even going to have a horse of my own. I'll work it out, just like we somehow found the trail that led to T.H."

For a few moments, they simply lay still beneath the soaring mass of stars. A sliver of moon rose in the rich black east, seeming to float above the earth.

"A cloak of diamonds," whispered Tony.

"Thought you said sequins."

"I was wrong. I'm beginning to get an inkling of how precious the universe is, not to mention some of the people in it. I guess there were even a few decent ones in my old neighborhood in the Bronx. I just left the area too soon and too young to really appreciate them."

Faith was silent for a moment, then rolled onto her elbow and leaned close to plant a feathery kiss on his brow.

But Tony wanted more. He reached for Faith, wanting to fully possess her intoxicating softness, her warmth. It was selfish, he knew—considering how he couldn't give her a commitment and all—but he couldn't help himself. She didn't pull away when he cradled her against him and stroked the satin of her hair.

"If I was gonna love someone, it would be you," he said, evading the truth in his own heart.

"I told you it wasn't necessary for you to make any declarations."

"It's been so fast. Barely two days."

He kissed her forehead, touched her cheek, drank in the sweetness of her breath. He ran his fingertips lightly across her lips, wishing he could touch her soul. But he shouldn't.

"We're probably all wrong for each other," he concluded.

He wasn't an easy man to live with, and much as he loved his profession, it was demanding and difficult. The world of Thoroughbred horse racing was a roller coaster of highs and lows, the latter sometimes devastating. His hours were long and irregular; he never really had days off. The situation would be hard on any wife or family.

Wife? With shock, Tony realized he was actually considering commitment. Which scared him, but not enough to pull away.

And he still longed to be truthful. "I don't think I'm your cowboy, Faith."

"Shh." She pressed a finger against his mouth. Then she replaced it with her lips, kissing him softly at first, then harder and more fervently.

He responded by molding her body against his, running his hand the length of her pliant spine. The little sounds of pleasure she made deep in her throat, the way she rocked her hips against his, turned him on even more. Soon he couldn't get enough of her, wanted to tear her clothes off, delve into her core....

They were both breathing so hard, it took him a moment to realize that loud voices and laughter were coming from the deserted farm's barn. He raised his head to listen.

"Damn it, what's going on?" he asked in a harsh whisper.

Faith was also alert. "I don't know." She was still breathing hard. "Is T.H. in danger?"

"I've gotta go see." He rose to his feet and approached the barbed-wire fence to climb over it.

"Be careful."

He would try his best. Just knowing that she was waiting for him would lighten his footsteps and temper the fierce anger that could get him into trouble.

At last he'd finally met a human being who seemed to be as trustworthy as a horse.

Trust. Tony simply couldn't find it within himself to believe that a woman could be true to him, would stick by him.

At least, that's what Faith believed.

Not that she regretted telling him she loved him, she thought, as she tried to peer through the darkness into which he'd disappeared. She'd said it and she'd meant it with all her heart. She even suspected Tony loved her a little, as well, or he wouldn't have kept pressing her to put voice to those feelings in the first place.

But they very likely *weren't* right for each other. And there was no way for them to tell, anyhow, since they'd only known each other two days.

Two days. Forty-eight hours during which Faith had faced past fears, reencountered her old dreams, returned to her past and reenvisioned her future. She ought to be feeling mixed up and slightly crazy, rather than deeply calm at her center.

About everything but Tony, that was. No matter what she'd told him about not having to make declarations, her heart wrenched a little every time she realized that things between her and Tony probably weren't going to work out.

She'd never been in love before....

Then again, she didn't have time to worry about personal issues right at this moment, Faith told herself, not when she wasn't even sure if Tony would return to the cornfield safely.

Feeling a bit chilled, she sneaked back into the corn rows to pick up Mrs. Sawyer's blanket. She also found the bag of food and the thermos. Good thing the sandwiches the woman had made were wrapped in plastic, since cornfields abounded with both rodents and insects. Throwing the blanket around herself, she sat back down near the fence.

Barely a minute later, a shadowy form appeared.

She rose to her knees. "Tony?"

"Yeah," he muttered, his voice rising with a curse as he crossed the fence. The barbed wire had obviously gotten him. "Don't talk so loud. And you shouldn't have assumed it was me. It could've been one of them and you'd have been caught."

"What happened?"

Again he cursed, this time sounding frustrated. "There's four of them now, having some damned beer and a poker party under the trees right in front of the barn."

"Four?" With those odds, they might have no chance at all.

"There's another pickup parked by the blue one. I think Zak invited some friends over. They've got a table and a camp lantern."

"I only hope those other guys are just friends, rather than more cohorts in the kidnapping."

"Let's be positive—George likes to hire on the cheap whenever he can. I don't tell him how many or how good the help is in my barn or he'd demand I cut pennies. Hobson isn't being paid that well, and he's probably stupid and flaky enough to play around on his employer's time. The new guys should be gone before morning."

"How about T.H.?"

"Couldn't see him. The only barn door we could get to is closed. They've propped a big, rusty piece of machinery against the door on the opposite side." Tony sat down beside her and took a swig from the thermos when she handed it to him. "After the friends leave, somebody's bound to fall asleep. Daybreak'll be the best time to hit them."

She was discouraged by the new development. "So you think Hobson is flaky and stupid and poorly paid?"

"George was obviously going to trip himself up some way. I just want to get T.H. away before you-know-what hits the fan."

She rummaged in the bag. "Want some cookies?"

"Sure. Then we should really try to catch some sleep. We need to be up at the crack of dawn."

She could tell he was peering at her in the darkness.

"Is that the blanket you've got on?" he asked. "Can we share it?"

Feeling a thrill, she moved closer and offered him an edge. Munching on a cookie, he snuggled in beside her, sliding an arm about her shoulders. But their interaction seemed drained of the passion they'd heated up before their rude interruption. Faith couldn't help feeling disappointed.

As if he knew what she was thinking, Tony angled his head to kiss her. She closed her eyes, parted her lips, only to have him cut the kiss short and pull away.

"We could kiss all night and more, but I don't want to make love with you unless I can offer you more than a roll in the hay."

Which reminded Faith of the fantasy she'd had at the Sawyer farm, though this time it wasn't funny. She tried to joke, anyway. "A roll in the cornfield. Get your crops straight, lover-boy."

"Yeah, I'm some lover-boy all right."

They settled back on the grass beside the fence. Though her emotions were awhirl, her mind restless, Faith could feel exhaustion settling in her limbs. It wouldn't be difficult to fall asleep lying beside Tony, no matter the effect he had on her hormones. He was probably right about their not making love unless they intended to get serious. Still, she couldn't help believing this would be the only chance she might ever get to become intimate with the man she loved.

Her feelings bittersweet—for she couldn't help but realize their adventure was about to end, not to mention their personal closeness—she snuggled into Tony's warmth and stared up at the stars, listening to his breathing mingled with the rhythm of the surrounding night's insects. Then she let her eyelids drift closed, knowing she needed to sleep.

For who knew what they'd have to deal with the next day?

"Damn it, the sun's been up for an hour already!" Tony rolled out of their cozy blanket and glared at the brilliant eastern sky. He slung on his binoculars. "I've got to see what's going on."

Faith blinked woozily, and while Tony sneaked off through the cornfield, she sat up and forced herself to focus on the rescue. Thank goodness Tony returned in a minute with good news.

"That second pickup is gone."

"Wonderful. We're back to two men instead of four."

"But the blue job is missing, too."

"Maybe there's no one here at all." Excited by the thought, she struggled to her feet, ignoring her protesting back, sore from the hardness of the ground. "Except T.H."

"We couldn't get that lucky. Even Hobson wouldn't be stupid enough to leave the horse unguarded." Hyper, he searched the area. "Where's the baseball bat? And the rope I dropped last night? Geez, the other man could be back any minute!"

Which concerned Faith. "You've never explained our strategy."

"We're gonna head for the barn from two separate directions." He pointed. "Follow the fence line and come back from over there. I'll go the shorter way and find the guard—knock him for a loop."

"Wouldn't it be better if I created a distraction? Made some noise?"

"No way. You're not gonna take the chance of getting shot."

But she determined to herself that she'd make some noise if there was reason for it—like Tony getting himself into a pinch. Surely Hobson or his cohort wouldn't shoot a woman on sight. She might even try batting her eyes to distract them.

"Try to get into the barn and untie T.H.," Tony was going on. "And be careful. He can be a handful. Might be a little crazy after what he's been through. He's not a farm horse, you know. Speak soft. Call him 'buddy.'"

"I'll deal with him," she said determinedly.

"As soon as you get hold of him, lead him out the door. I should be there in a second to help." Glancing at her with a frown, Tony added, "He nips sometimes, but he's usually trying to be playful."

"I've been bitten by a horse before." And she'd gladly suffer a bruise to free the kidnapped animal.

They crossed the fence, Faith showing Tony how to pull on the sagging barbed wire, holding it to the ground with their feet. He paid close attention, no doubt gauging how difficult it was going to be to get T.H. over and into the cornfield.

Ready to split up, Tony surprised Faith by taking her in his arms for a hug. "Be careful, Mary Poppins."

Noting the emotion in his dark eyes made her adrenaline surge. "You, too, Tony. But don't worry, we're going to win."

Then she was off, bending slightly to remain low on the horizon, keeping to the tall weeds near the fence. Passing a copse of raggedy fir trees, she scooted through the shade beneath their heavy limbs... and almost fell when her sneakered foot rolled on the handle of an old, abandoned tool.

The handle was sturdy and heavy, having once been a hoe or a rake. Deciding she could use it as a weapon, Faith picked it up and dusted off the dirt, then continued her furtive journey. Slipping through more weeds, she finally approached the barn.

That's when she heard the yells and a cracking sound that could only be a gunshot. "Tony!"

Her heart in her throat, she ran forward, still trying to keep out of sight by ducking behind a tree, then some bushes. Up ahead, near a shed, she spotted a tall man standing over someone on the ground. As she came closer, she also saw the gun in the man's hand, his reddish hair. Hobson! And he'd obviously shot Tony!

Without thinking, Faith sped out of her cover, swinging the long tool handle like a club. Hobson had only enough time for a surprised expression before she hit his face for all she was worth.

Blood spurted from his nose and he dropped the gun. "Ya-ah!"

"Get him, Faith!"

Tony was alive...and struggling to his feet.

Faith smacked Hobson a second time, making the man stagger backward. Tony was just in time to slam the bat across the back of Hobson's head. He dropped hard and fast.

"Tony!" Faith ran to him, appalled at the dark red stain spreading from a wound in his thigh. "You've been shot!" And for the first time since meeting Tony, she starting crying.

They clung together, and he kissed the top of her head. "Come on, come on. I'm hurt, but I'm not dying."

Though she could tell he was in pain. He winced every time he moved. If the shot had done more damage...if it had hit a vital organ...if it had killed Tony...

Faith realized she could have lost him for good!

Unable to stand the thought, she wept harder, especially when she realized that even though he'd survive the gunshot wound, he would be leaving her soon. She would merely lose him in another way.

That he'd be alive was the important part, she told herself.

"It's only a flesh wound," Tony said, appearing uncomfortable as she nodded and sobbed at the same time. "The bullet went right through." He glanced at Hobson. "Damn jerk caught sight of me before I could nail him. I'm gonna tie him up. Go get T.H. and bring him here. Get him out of the barn as fast as you can. No telling when the other guy will be back."

Chapter Ten

Get T.H. out of the barn as fast as you can.

Tony's words echoing through her head, Faith sprinted for the building, unfastened the door, then, at the last minute, halted before opening it. Horses were easily spooked and picked up on their handler's feelings. She let her breathing slow, forced herself to relax and searched for that calm center now lost somewhere inside her.

The process was far more difficult this time than last. She'd told Tony she loved him but that she hadn't expected any declaration from him. So she'd thought at the time. But the euphoria she'd felt at realizing she was in love had been short-lived—and for the very reason that he *hadn't* confessed his love in return. She wasn't as independent as she liked to think. She wanted Tony, needed him.

And he needed her, she reminded herself . . . to get his horse.

When she figured she had herself as together as she was going to be, Faith pulled the heavy wooden door open, letting it lean against the side of the barn. Inside, thin strips of sunlight from the cracks between the building's boards crisscrossed cobwebby shadows. The place smelled of stale manure and decades of dust. Crates and machinery littered the floor and an ancient horse collar hung on one wall, a stiff-looking bridle looped over it.

But Faith's eyes were drawn to the centerpiece of the scene, the chestnut colt. True Heart snorted softly, raising his finely shaped head to stare at the new intruder. His large, dark eyes glimmered, his ears pricked above the white star on his forehead. Powerful muscles flexed beneath a gleaming coat of deep copper and gold. His expression alert, his posture proud, the product of hundreds of years of selective breeding, he seemed to know he was a blue-blooded prince who was being held captive in a seedy dungeon.

And Faith was the only one who could rescue him. When the colt snorted again, she was moved to action, quickly noting the ratty piece of rope that tied the horse's halter to a peg on the barn wall. From the looks of it, she suspected T.H. had been chewing on his makeshift lead, and she feared he would get away if she led him outside. One jerk of his powerful head could easily snap the rope in two.

She glanced about, her gaze settling on the old horse collar and bridle. Laying the tool handle she'd been carrying against the wall, she reached up for the bridle. The hard leather squeaked, and she had to brush dirt off before she could untangle the reins and straighten the rusty bit.

Then she approached T.H., keeping the bridle close to her side. "Hi, buddy," she crooned softly. "How're you doing? Tony's waiting outside for you." As if the horse could understand.... But, talking to calm both herself and T.H., she went on, "We need to get you out of here. Please behave yourself. We want to save your life."

The colt remained still, watching her. And when she got near enough, yet too far away for him to nip her easily, she leaned closer to do the usual trick she'd always employed with strange horses—she blew in his nostrils.

T.H. didn't seem to mind. His nose fluttered, taking in her scent. Then she reached out to pet those velvety nostrils, continuing to make murmuring, soothing sounds. The colt was so busy listening and smelling that he hardly realized she'd stuck the bit between his lips. And when he objected to that, tossing his head as she secured the bit, she'd already gotten the bridle up over his ears.

T.H. snorted loudly now and tossed his head some more, trying to chew on the bit and acting like he wanted to rear.

Faith tried to keep him down, held on to the reins for dear life. "I know, I know. It's an awful old bridle." And it didn't look very fancy smashed down over his halter as it was. "But it'll have to do, buddy." She untied the rope. "We've got to get you out of here."

Get T.H. out of the barn as fast as you can.

Following some unconscious step of internal logic, Faith leapt onto a nearby crate, threw the rope and the reins over the horse's neck and slid onto his back. As she had when riding bareback on Cochise, she gripped the horse with her legs and urged him toward the open door.

But T.H. was no calm farm horse.

Faith suddenly remembered that as he shot out of the building as if he were leaving a starting gate. The ground flew by in a blur.

Frightened, she pulled on the reins and tried to slow the colt down. "Whoa!"

But he was far too strong and now had the bit in his teeth, probably wild with the scent of freedom after days of being cooped up. Faith flashed on him running himself into the barbed-wire fence or stepping into a hole and breaking his leg.

He could kill both himself and his rescuer—what horrible irony that would be!

Grasping his coarse mane with one hand and his rippling hide with her legs, struggling to keep her seat, Faith pulled back on the reins and shouted again, "Whoa, buddy!"

T.H. hesitated, slowing slightly. At the same time, a man with shaggy hair and a mustache appeared out of nowhere to lunge at the horse.

"Stay away!" Faith yelled at Zak Hobson's partner. But the man already had a hand on the bridle. T.H. stopped but tried to rear, Faith clutching his neck. Still, she managed to kick at the mustached guy.

"I said stay away!"

He slapped at her sneakered foot and snarled, "Get off that horse, you little witch!"

While Faith lashed at the man with the reins, True Heart wheeled, squealing low in his throat. He kicked out with a back leg, and Faith winced as shod metal thudded against flesh. The mustached man grunted and sprawled to the ground, groaning and cursing.

Turning the colt in the direction of the shed where she'd left Tony, Faith was thankful when T.H. took off at a lope instead of a gallop. The bushes and trees they passed must have hidden her violent encounter or, she figured, Tony would have been shouting at her.

She found him standing, leaning against the shed to keep his weight off his hurt leg. Even in pain, he smiled broadly when he saw the horse.

"Hey, buddy, good to see you again...alive." Then he glanced at Faith, looking surprised. "You rode him bareback? Are you crazy?"

"You said to get him out of the barn as fast as I could. And his lead is in bad condition."

Tony clucked to the colt and pushed away from the shed to grasp the reins Faith tossed him. "Hey, hey, buddy, how you doing?"

As the horse pranced around, basking in Tony's attention, Faith slid off, nearly falling when her legs acted as if they were made of rubber. She wasn't sure if that was due more to her rusty riding skills or to the frightening situation.

She motioned behind her. "T.H. kicked the heck out of Hobson's friend. He's flat on the ground back there." She also noticed Hobson himself lying nearby, neatly tied up with the rope.

"Let's hit the road...and fast." Tony started hobbling. "Just in case the friend gets up or somebody else happens along."

Faith couldn't help but be concerned at how weak he seemed, how pale. "You can't walk. Get on T.H. and I'll lead him."

"I'm okay," he said tightly.

"No, you're not."

"Then wait until we cross the fence."

What could she do with such a stubborn man? Nothing, Faith realized, once again reminded of how close she was to losing Tony. If only they had more time together...if only time could do the trick. For Faith knew she was all wrong for Tony D'Angelo.

She guessed she just didn't dream big enough for a man like him.

They approached the fence, but T.H. didn't particularly like the look of the barbed wire, even when it was lying on the ground. He snorted and jumped around a bit, but between Tony and Faith, they finally coaxed him across. Once in the cornfield, however, he settled down and let them lead him along a row.

Faith stopped as soon as they'd gotten several yards into the tall stalks. "Now you've got to ride," she ordered Tony, hoping he would think her concern was strictly over his wound and not over her own heart. She wouldn't pin that guilt trip on him. "You've lost too much blood."

His face seemed even paler. With some help from her, he managed to struggle onto the colt's back and lean forward to cling to his neck.

"I'm really worried. You should go to a hospital."

"No way." He made a face. "The bullet didn't hit an artery or anything. I'm not gonna bleed to death. Besides, I've got some stuff in the truck to help fix me up." Tony patted T.H. "If we get there, that is. I hope my buddy doesn't get spooked with all these crackling leaves and throw me off."

"He won't." Faith stared into the horse's liquid dark eyes and addressed him directly, urgently. "Will you, buddy? You know Tony loves you and he's come all this way to get you. You don't want to hurt him."

Then she took the reins and led T.H. forward, half expecting the trainer to say something sarcastic about her mushiness. When there wasn't a peep out of him, she became even more worried about his condition.

Tony felt like his leg was on fire, but he forced himself to keep a stiff upper lip. Otherwise, he knew Faith would strong-arm him into a hospital whether he liked it or not.

Once they'd loaded T.H. and tied him at the back of the truck, Tony unpacked the first-aid kit he always carried and allowed Faith to clean his wound. She tore at the bullet hole in his pants, making it larger, then applied peroxide to his leg with a big cotton ball. She tried to be gentle, but it hurt like hell. He swallowed a yelp of pain, hoping she didn't notice the tears that sprang in his eyes.

"There's some antibiotic cream in there," he told her, shaky, motioning to the kit. "Why don't you put some of that on next?"

She examined the tube with a frown. "This is for horses, isn't it?"

"Yeah, but it'll work on me, too. Hope you can drive a stick shift, because we need to take off."

"I know how to drive tractors, not to mention trucks."

She helped him into the vehicle and climbed up to the driver's seat, sparing one last, concerned look for him before starting up.

Then she put the truck in reverse, pulled out on the road, switched gears and rumbled off. Tony leaned back, holding on to the edge of the seat. A couple of miles down, they passed Myron Sawyer's farm and saw the man leaning against the fence. A tractor was parked in the driveway. Sawyer spotted the truck in turn and waved.

Tony gave the man a thumbs-up sign. From the side mirror, he watched the farmer climb onto the tractor, then pull it across the road, trailing a big piece of machinery and, behind that, a couple of wagons. Sawyer drove the tractor directly down into the ditch on the opposite side of his farm buildings, stopping so the machinery was dead center of the road.

Faith gazed into her own side mirror. "What on earth is he doing with that combine and the wagons?"

"Blocking the road. In case Hobson or his friend decide to chase us." Tony smiled with satisfaction. "It was his idea—he told me before we left. And I guess he's got a pal shutting the road off in the opposite direction—Mrs. Sawyer's making the call right now. There's no way those guys can catch up with us unless they have an airplane or can travel overland.''

"So that's what you two were cooking up." She glanced at him accusingly. "And you were being so careful that I wouldn't hear. Did you think I couldn't keep a secret or something?''

"I wanted to limit your involvement, that's all. Something I tried to do from the first." And failed.

Just as he'd failed to limit his own emotional involvement with her. Tony stared at Faith, light brown hair blown back into a halo from the wind streaming through the window, intent features as clear-cut and beautiful as an angel's. She'd admitted she loved him, and, God help him, he'd realized somewhere along the line that he loved her. He simply couldn't help himself.

She'd begun this journey by coming to see his horse, and she'd gotten his heart, as well.

Though that still didn't mean he had much to offer her—certainly not marriage. There was no way he could even consider subjecting Faith to his kind of life-style. Besides, he might be feeling this way because of their success, but he knew he'd be back to his old cynical ways in a few weeks, maybe a few days. He wasn't good at intimate relationships; his personality was too harsh for a sweet, loving woman like Faith.

Brooding once again on his hectic, gypsy life-style and the past that continued to tarnish his present, Tony felt so much sorrow, it came out in a huge sigh.

Faith glanced at him worriedly. "Are you all right?''

He realized his heartsickness was probably making him look physically ill. "Actually, my leg is feeling better." Which was the truth. "I was sighing in relief.''

"We aren't quite out of the woods yet, though. I assume you want me to head for Chicago?''

"Right. The police won't be looking for this truck, so we should make it. Keep to the main highway and head for Dubuque, then we'll cut over into Illinois." He glanced back through the truck's rear window and saw T.H. moving around. "We should stop somewhere and give my buddy some water and a little hay. Not to mention get that excuse for a bridle off him. Where did you find it, anyway?"

"In the barn on that farm. It's old."

"And stiff," he added. "Though I can see why you used it instead of the cruddy rope they had him on. I'll cut off one of the reins and use that as a lunge line."

Concentrating on the horse kept his mind off more personal problems for the next twenty or so miles. He told Faith about the promise he'd seen in the colt from the very beginning and shared stories of T.H.'s progress and his own training strategies. As he'd expected, she was interested in every detail and asked intelligent questions.

As soon as they reached the bluffs of Dubuque and coasted down to cross the great girdered bridge that spanned the Mississippi, he suggested once again that they stop.

"I want to make T.H. more comfortable."

"We should also look at your leg, maybe clean out the wound again and apply more antibiotic."

He grimaced and tried to joke. "You just wanna hurt me, don't you?"

"I have to get even some way," she teased. "I'll never forget being tied up and thrown in a stall."

They both laughed, though Tony didn't feel especially amused. How long was it going to take them to get back to Chicago? Four hours—maybe more—with this old, cranky truck? Then he'd have to find some way to say goodbye and would probably never see her again.

He was tempted to take a rest stop at every turn to delay the inevitable.

Once in Illinois, Faith stopped at a service station to fill the bucket with water and buy some junk food and soda for herself and Tony. He didn't get out for fear a customer or attendant would see his bloody leg. T.H. also might spook at the traffic and noise.

Farther down the road, they found a grassy area where they could pull over and check out the colt. Ignoring his own pain, Tony climbed in the back of the truck, took off the bridle and gave T.H. some water and hay, careful the horse didn't eat too much, too fast and make himself sick. Then he had Faith hold on to the rope attached to the halter while he ran his hands up and down each of the horse's legs.

"No heat. I can't believe our good luck. I think he's okay."

Faith stroked the colt's shining neck. "Thank goodness, poor guy."

T.H. nickered and chewed on Tony's shirtsleeve.

"Aw, isn't that cute?" said Faith.

"Real cute." But Tony wasn't too macho to straighten and give the colt a great big kiss on the nose. "Glad to have you back and in one piece, buddy. Of course," he told Faith, "I'm gonna order X rays and a complete examination when we get back to Rolling Meadows.... I'll turn T.H. over to my assistant before the police get to me."

Her expression sobered. "I forgot about the police."

"Well, they're gonna be there and they'll probably take me into custody." Though they wouldn't be taking Faith if he could help it. "No problem, they won't be holding me long—not after I give them names, places and details."

Tony wanted the next item on the agenda to be cutting up the bridle, but Faith insisted on reexamining his thigh. Bringing the colt to the rear of the truck bed, Tony tied the rope to the latticework and climbed out to hobble over to the edge of the grassy area. He sat down on a tree stump he'd spotted there and prepared himself for pain.

"You don't have to screw up your face like that yet," she told him, sounding amused. "I haven't touched you."

He opened his eyes as a car whizzed by, a blur of metallic bronze. Then, to his surprise, he heard the squeal of brakes.

Cotton ball in one hand, peroxide in the other, Faith paused to stare. "It's doing a U-turn and coming back."

"Help me up, will you?"

He took the hand she offered and was standing when the bronze car pulled in behind the truck. Fearing some sort of authority had caught up with them, Tony was relieved to recognize Harlan Crandall's Mercedes.

The owner got out, a worried look on his face.

"Hey, Harlan," called Tony, limping toward him. "I can't believe you found us."

"Neither can I," the owner said tightly.

Harlan's cool tone made Tony think twice, something he should have been doing the moment he'd identified the car. After all, why had the man been heading for Dubuque... unless he'd known where T.H. was being held in the first place?

Tony glanced around, realizing he had no weapon.

But it was already too late. The owner pulled a gun from inside his jacket.

"You stupid fool. You had to stick your nose into this, didn't you?" Then Harlan ordered, "Raise your hands." He gazed at Faith. "You too, missy."

Beads of nervous sweat stood out on the man's balding brow. When Faith moved, shifting her stance, he pointed the gun at her.

"Stand still... or I'll kill you right on the spot, I swear I will!"

Which aroused Tony's protective instincts. He moved forward, placing himself in front of her. "Hey, shoot me if you want to, but leave her alone."

Harlan stepped back toward the truck at the aggressive gesture, his eyes staring and fevered, his hands shaking slightly. He was totally freaked out.

Tony decided to continue the offensive, not that he could do a good job of attacking Harlan physically, considering the shape he was in. Not unless he could get a lot closer.

"What's the matter with you, anyway, Harlan? How could you do something like this?"

"How could I do it? What choice did I have? My company's being bought out and I'm going bankrupt." Harlan's voice climbed a couple of octaves, nearly cracking. "Though everything would have been all right if you hadn't gotten yourself involved."

"And T.H. would be dead," muttered Faith.

Harlan scowled. "Who *is* she, anyway?"

"My girlfriend." Tony tried to think fast, hoping to keep the man distracted while he inched forward a bit more. "But let's get back to you." Might as well find out as much as he could in case they got out of this. "So you were going to collect on the insurance, huh?"

"And George's half of the ransom."

"But you found some pretty flaky accomplices, didn't you?"

"Flaky? They were dolts, idiots! They didn't contact me when they were supposed to. I couldn't contact them—"

"Because they were having too much fun playing poker, swilling beer with friends." Tony inched forward yet again. "Lots of people in Dubuque County know about T.H., Harlan. And we already traced the license plate of the trailer to you. You might as well give yourself up."

Harlan's lip curled. "And go to jail? No thank you."

"Then maybe you'd better take off for South America."

"I'll figure out how to cover up...after I kill you and your cute little friend. You've made me far too angry." Now Harlan seemed to realize Tony was almost within striking distance. He backed up, coming within a foot or so of the rear of the truck. The muzzle of his little automatic was aimed directly at Tony's chest.

Still, Tony prepared himself for a leap at the gun, felt his adrenaline surge. But before he got the chance, he heard a sharp snap—the rope gave—and out of the truck came T.H.'s head snaking along. His teeth were bared.

And Harlan screamed as the colt bit down hard on his shoulder. At the same time, Tony leapt for the man's gun hand. The weapon went flying into the air, and Faith went after it. Tony knocked the older man down, straddled him and punched him. Would have hit him again if Harlan had shown any fight. Instead, the owner just lay there moaning and groaning.

"Relax, Tony. I have a bead on him."

Faith. She firmly trained the gun on Harlan.

"Guess you know how to use one of those, too," Tony remarked, not surprised.

"My dad taught me how to shoot, in case a rabid skunk wandered onto the farm."

"Yeah, this one's both rabid and a skunk!" Tony took hold of the truck and pulled himself up. "Can you climb into the back here and tie up my buddy again?" A short piece of the rope remained. Meanwhile, he patted T.H. to keep the horse calm. "Then hand me the bridle and that knife in the bigger canvas bag, okay? We need to tie up this dirtbag, then make a lunge line."

Faith handed the gun to Tony and did as he asked.

Tony threatened Harlan as the older man sat up. "I'm gonna put you in the back with T.H., let him chew on you and stomp you all the way back to Chicago—how do you like that?''

"My God, no!" Harlan appeared truly terrified. "That horse has always hated me! He'll kill me!"

Actually, Tony was merely taunting him, though it seemed appropriate to let T.H. have his revenge on the corrupt owner. Harlan would have gladly sacrificed T.H. for his own ambitions. And he would have killed Tony and Faith for rescuing the horse and ruining his plans.

Taking the gun and watching Tony saw off the bridle's reins, Faith mused, "It was Harlan that T.H. tried to nip after the Kentucky Derby, wasn't it?"

"Yeah, that horse knows a bad apple when he sees one." Just as Tony knew a good woman when he finally found her.

His heart was going to break when he had to let her go.

Chapter Eleven

Immediately upon returning to Rolling Meadows Race-course, Tony notified track security, the local authorities and George Langley of True Heart's recovery and their capture of the man responsible.

Faith underwent hours of questioning by the police and the FBI in the shedrow's tight, airless office before they told her she was off the hook and could leave. George Langley chose that moment to arrive and immediately demanded to see his horse. Tony sent his assistant with Langley, and at last they were alone. Faith was a nervous wreck. Her tiny apartment in the crowded city suddenly seemed like a haven to her. She was exhausted, both physically and emotionally, and she wanted to get her goodbyes over with as quickly as possible.

"I guess that's it, then," she said to Tony, looking for something in his veiled expression, some sign that she meant more to him than a companion in getting back his horse.

"That's it," he echoed, his voice rougher than usual. And he was staring at her intently. "You're free to go."

What if she didn't want to? Not that she would tell him so. She wouldn't be one of those clingy, teary women who wouldn't let a man walk away from her when he was ready.

She would mourn him, instead, in private.

"Yeah, I guess I should get home." She forced a grin she wasn't feeling. "Lucy's going to be awful mad as it is."

"Lucy?"

"My cat, remember? Audra's been taking care of her, but Lucy owns *me*...."

Her words trailed off. She wasn't even up to joking. She had a lump the size of a bale of hay stuck in her throat, and her eyes were stinging. She looked away from the face that had become precious to her in a few short days and saw a suburban taxi drive up to stop outside the nearby gate.

"I, uh, called the taxi for you," Tony said. "Don't worry, the barn'll pay for the ride into the city."

"Oh."

Part of her wasn't surprised, but another part had hoped that he would at least drive her home himself after all they'd been through, after all they'd shared. Obviously, she didn't even mean as much to Tony as True Heart.

He walked her to the gate and out to the taxi. The driver stuck his head out the window. "This the ride to the city?"

"You got it," Tony said, pulling a couple of twenties from his shirt pocket and handing it to the guy. "This should cover it." Then Tony shoved her into the back seat with a brisk "See you around," leaving Faith feeling more hurt than she could bear.

Yeah, sure thing.

She hadn't expected any sweet words and promises, but the man could have taken a little more time with her. She'd told him she loved him and that she didn't expect anything back. Not that that hadn't turned out to be a load...

Still, he should have had the decency to leave her with a warm embrace, if not one last kiss.

Faith saw Tony watch the taxi as the driver did a U-turn and headed back down the road. She felt like a kid with her nose pressed to the glass of a candy counter. What she wanted was on the other side, but she couldn't quite get to it.

Tony grew smaller... and smaller... and finally turned away. Faith settled in the back seat, hoping she could keep her emotions in check on the long ride back to the city. No sense in making a fool of herself in front of a stranger. She'd already done that with Tony D'Angelo.

Her only consolation was that at least she hadn't been another notch on his bedpost.

"Kentucky Derby winner True Heart is safe and sound and will soon be back in training at Rolling Meadows Race-course," said the television news announcer as the camera focused on T.H. hanging his head over the webbing in front of his stall.

Faith wasn't sure she wanted to see more, when the picture switched to a shot of Tony walking outside the barn. But the camera didn't stay there; it came back to the face of the announcer as he went over the details of the kidnapping again.

In briefer detail, thank goodness.

She'd even appeared on television herself, as well as in all the newspapers—an uncomfortable situation, which had forced her to do some fast talking at Pilgrim Insurance. Explaining that Tony D'Angelo was a good friend, that she'd felt compelled to help him, she'd gotten them to write off her week's absence as vacation days but had been warned that she'd better not do anything that crazy again.

Oh, well. She didn't intend to stay with the insurance company, anyway, planned to quit as soon as the school loans she'd applied for came through. Hopeful that she could make her dreams come true now, she'd changed her mind about getting into debt and was going to finish school in one fell swoop of a semester.

"Then we're going to blow this dirty old city," she told Lucy, who'd leapt up beside her on the couch. She cuddled the cat and rubbed her face against the soft calico fur. "I'll get a job in the far suburbs where I can take you out in the yard. Maybe I'll start up my own business." She smiled. "And someday I'll get us a horse. What kind do you want? An Appaloosa? A palomino? A chestnut?"

As if Lucy could care. The cat would no doubt hiss and puff herself up at the sight of any horse, including True Heart.

True Heart.

Tony D'Angelo.

Once again, Faith tried to push aside her sad feelings, the awful hurt of Tony packing her into that darned taxi and not even calling her in nearly three days.

Letting Lucy squirm away, Faith rose to shut off the television and do some straightening up. Exhausted from the trip, she'd done little the past few days except lay around and sleep, make reassuring phone calls to her family and eat the "healthy" food Audra had insisted on dropping by. A strict vegetarian and no cook, her neighbor couldn't make—and didn't believe in—chicken soup. But Audra thought that bean-curd broth from the weird little deli on the corner was equally curative, as well as other Oriental-type dishes, frozen yogurt and cheesecake.

Throwing out a carton that held Japanese noodles and tofu, Faith smiled at the way Audra had been fussing over her. To keep her neighbor from getting into trouble with Pilgrim Insurance, she'd told the police she'd remembered the license plate in its entirety and hadn't mentioned Audra's not-so-official assistance in tracking it down.

When the doorbell rang, Faith thought it was her neighbor again, asking what she wanted for dessert tonight. She pushed the intercom button. "Yes?"

"Yippee-ti-yi-yo," said a familiar gravelly voice.

Faith froze, her heart nearly stopping. "Tony?"

"Yeah, where are you?"

"The fourth floor, second apartment on the left wing."

"So let me in."

Her finger trembled as she pressed the door buzzer. What the heck was he doing here?

Panicked, she ran to her closet to pull out a skirt and a sweater. Changing out of her T-shirt and jeans, wishing she had more time to prepare herself, she ran a brush through her wild-looking hair, then swiped on some lipstick. She realized the pink mess was smudged as she heard the knock. Grabbing a tissue, she wiped her lips before opening the door.

"Wow, you look beautiful."

Faith couldn't respond, simply stared, searching for words.

Not that Tony wasn't as handsome as usual, but she'd never seen him dressed this way. Wearing leather chaps over jeans and cowboy boots, he'd added a wide-brimmed Stetson, which he now removed with a flourish.

"Nice duds, huh?"

Heart in her throat, she croaked, "Kind of unusual for you," and wondered what it all meant.

"Got into a cowboy mood." He came inside, his dark eyes assessing her face. "Wanna ride off into the sunset with me?"

"The sunset?" A thrill shot through her. Could he really mean he wanted to do more than just see her? "Ride off where? On some kind of horse trip?"

"Not unless you'd like to do a dude ranch for a honeymoon." He tossed his hat aside and reached for her, pulling her to him. "I'm talking marriage. I'm proposing, all right?"

Her mouth dropped open. "Marriage?"

"Yeah, I know I've never exactly been a straight-shooter, a hero in a white hat, but I'm willing to work at it."

"Marriage?" she repeated. Tony must be serious or he wouldn't be dressed this way. Part of her was thrilled, but on another level, a deeper one, she suddenly felt the flare of righteous anger. And jerked away. "You're unbelievable, Tony. You stick me into a taxi one day without so much as a fare-thee-well and then show up talking marriage, probably expecting me to fall all over you!"

"That would be nice." His grin was lopsided.

Though she could tell he was uncomfortable. "Well, it's not that easy. We have to talk." She crossed her arms. "What have you been doing for the past few days—making up your mind?"

"So to speak. Trying to figure out if I could do right by you." He glanced around, as if attempting to relieve the tension. "Cozy place. Sort of small, though." He turned back to her. "How would you like something bigger? Like a town house? You could stay there while you finish your degree, then either travel with me, maybe assist me and exercise the horses, or you could manage the lay-up and training farm I bought near Dubuque."

Her mind spun. "A farm?"

"Yeah, I got some acres from Sawyer. Paid him better than the going rate. Figured it was the least I could do, since he wouldn't take any money for that truck. Besides, Iowa is home for you, right?"

"You bought the farm because of me?" Now she was sincerely touched. "But we need to talk about feelings, Tony."

"Feelings?" He gazed at her with such intensity, she felt ripples of electricity resonate throughout her body. "Fine,

I've got plenty of those—you've been making my guts go
around and around since the first time I saw you. I wanted
you then. I want you now.... I would have taken you if I
thought I'd be any good for you."

Keeping herself from melting straight into his arms, she
asked, "So what changed your mind?"

"You. Your outlook on the world. I realized I'm a different kind of guy than I'd always thought. I'm not as bad
as I feared. You and your belief in humanity has kinda
changed my opinion—even of myself. If I keep working at
it, maybe I'll deserve a woman like you."

Her mouth trembled and tears threatened to fill her eyes.
"A woman like what? The Mary Poppins sort?" She wasn't
sure she liked that.

He grinned. "Nah, the true-heart type, the kind who
never quits. If you had a second pair of legs, sweetheart, I'd
put you in the Derby."

True heart.

Now, she liked *that.*

"I love you, Faith," Tony said softly, all cockiness flee-
ing, his face loaded with all the emotion she could ever
want.

This time, when he took her in his arms, she slid her
hands up his chest and gazed into his intense dark eyes. "I
love you, too." She touched his rugged face, ran her fingers
over the scar above his eyebrow and along the slightly
crooked nose.

"So this is a yes?" he asked, searching for her lips. Then
he tried very hard to scowl. "Or do I have to take you into
personal custody again?"

"Not necessary. I'm coming with you—fire, flood or
bullets." After all, love and marriage to an exciting, wonderful man was one of her highest dreams.

They were off for an adventure of a lifetime.

* * *

Two Months Later—The Breeder's Cup, Churchill Downs, Kentucky

"Doesn't T.H. look good?" Faith enthused to her husband during the post parade for the Breeder's Cup Classic, a one and a quarter mile, three-million-dollar race that attracted the cream of the Thoroughbred crop. "You'd hardly believe he went through all he did back in September."

Seated in the box seat between Faith and George Langley, Tony glanced at the program. "Yeah, but look at this—they only made him ten to one. What an insult!"

Tony took everything personally when it came to his horses, and T.H. was truly *his* horse now, as well as Faith's.

George Langley had been so happy to get the colt back, so upset over Harlan's betrayal, he'd rewarded T.H.'s rescuers with ten percent ownership. That was after he'd bought out Harlan, who'd needed the money for a good lawyer. Amelia Langley had also apologized all over herself, and George had assured Tony that his wife would be nice from now on or she wouldn't be coming to the track.

George had turned out to be okay, Tony thought, even if he was a worrywart.

"I'm so nervous, I could chew nails," George complained.

A case in point. But Tony nodded and pulled at his silk tie. "Me, too."

T.H. hadn't won since the first Saturday in May, hadn't had a real race to prepare him for this test since his kidnapping, had only placed in an allowance race and had shown some solid workouts. Yet he was going up against the most outstanding horses in the country.

But when Tony gazed down the track at his colt's competitors, he had to smile, admiring the shimmer of bay coats, dark browns, grays and coppery chestnuts as they paraded by.

"Look at those heroes—some athletes, huh?" he whispered to Faith, leaning over to slide an arm around her. "They ran their hearts out to get here. They risked life and limb to entertain the crowds." More than a thousand pounds skimming the earth on fragile legs with human-sized ankles. "If T.H. loses, at least he'll get beat by the best."

But Tony's hope was that T.H. wouldn't lose. He had this hunch. . . .

Still nervous, he tried to distract himself by glancing up at Myron Sawyer and his wife, seated some rows above. The farmer grinned and waved a win ticket. Tony gave him a thumbs-up sign.

Then he turned back to Faith. Wearing a softly draped dress and coat in a shade of blue to match her eyes, she looked beautiful. *Was* beautiful, inside and out. He could still hardly believe his luck in finding her. She was another plus T.H. had brought about, along with a name in the training profession.

"They're loading them up," said George, starting to fan himself anxiously with his program.

The man always did that, no matter the weather.

Tony shook his head and leaned forward just in time to see the gates open and a wall of horses come charging out.

Scandalous, Stan Berg's bay speedster, went straight to the lead, a couple of other horses moving up to keep him company. As usual, T.H. settled in at the back of the pack, dead last.

Tony watched the throng negotiate the clubhouse turn, then head down the backstretch. He noted the reasonably fast time. Would the horses up front tire themselves out enough for T.H. to pick them off at the end?

At least the chestnut colt was moving, coming up, passing horses as they approached the final turn. Legs driving like pistons, he entered the long Churchill stretch, looking strong, his nose pointed toward the finish line.

As one, the crowd *ahhed* and rose to their feet.

"He's not going to make it!" cried George.

"Oh, yes, he is!" yelled Faith.

Tony merely moved a raised arm in rhythm with the colt's stride. "Come on, buddy," he chanted. "Come on, come on. Against the odds, ten to one—prove them wrong."

T.H. came up on the last horse, Scandalous, keeping pace with him. But Berg's colt looked leg weary. And T.H. seemed to gather himself as if he were looking for something deep within. Then, with a final, powerful burst of speed, the chestnut shot forward, streaking across the finish line a bare length in front.

Once more he was a winner!

The crowd roared. George wept with joy... for the second time that year.

And Tony felt as if his smile would split his face in two as he and Faith, George and Amelia, made their way down to the winner's circle. Faith held Tony's hand.

"You won!" someone shouted as they passed by.

"Sure did." Tony drew Faith closer. She was his love, his anchor.

He'd won all right—more than anyone would ever know.

*   *   *   *   *

Dark secrets, dangerous desire...

Lovers DARK AND DANGEROUS

Three spine-tingling tales from the dark side of love.

This October, enter the world of shadowy romance as Silhouette presents the third in their annual tradition of thrilling love stories and chilling story lines. Written by three of Silhouette's top names:

LINDSAY McKENNA
LEE KARR
RACHEL LEE

Haunting a store near you this October.

Only from

Silhouette®
™

...where passion lives.

LDD

Take 4 bestselling love stories FREE

Plus get a FREE surprise gift!

BABY'S CHOICE

Those mischievous matchmaking babies are back, as Marie Ferrarella's Baby's Choice series continues in August with MOTHER ON THE WING (SR #1026).

Frank Harrigan could hardly explain his sudden desire to fly to Seattle. Sure, an old friend had written to him out of the blue, but there was something else.... Then he spotted Donna McCollough, or rather, she fell right into his lap. And from that moment on, they were powerless to interfere with what angelic fate had lovingly ordained.

Continue to share in the wonder of life and love, as babies-in-waiting handpick the most perfect parents, only in

R O M A N C E™

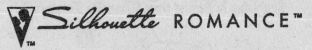
Silhouette ROMANCE™

First comes marriage.... Will love follow?
Find out this September when Silhouette Romance
presents

Hasty Weddings

Join six couples who marry for convenient reasons, and still
find happily-ever-afters. Look for these wonderful books by
some of your favorite authors:

Beginning in August from Silhouette Romance...

by Sandra Steffen

Three sexy, single brothers bet they'll never say "I do." But the Harris boys are about to discover their vows of bachelorhood don't stand a chance against the forces of love!

Don't miss:

BACHELOR DADDY (8/94): Single father Mitch Harris gets more than just parenting lessons from his lovely neighbor, Raine McAlister.

BACHELOR AT THE WEDDING (11/94): He caught the garter, she caught the bouquet. And Kyle Harris is in for more than a brief encounter with single mom Clarissa Cohagan.

EXPECTANT BACHELOR (1/95): Taylor Harris gets the shock of his life when the stunning Gina Jenson asks him to father her child.

Find out how these confirmed bachelors finally take the marriage plunge. Don't miss WEDDING WAGER, only from

Silhouette
R O M A N C E™

SRSS1